For Lisa,

Looking forward

An American Affair

to reading more

of your work,

Mark

An American Affair

Mark Brazaitis

Texas Review Press
Huntsville, Texas

FIRST EDITION, 2005

Requests for permission to reproduce material from this work should be sent
to:

Permissions
Texas Review Press
English Department
Sam Houston State University
Huntsville, TX 77341-2146

ACKNOWLEDGEMENTS

I am fortunate to have people in my life who support what I do in ways large
and larger. Some of these people are: my mother and step-father, Sheila Loftus and
Jim Eddinger; my father, Tom Brazaitis; my sister and brother-in-law, Sarah Brazaitis
and George Gushue; my cousins Frank and Maureen Greicius; my in-laws, John and
Jean Penn; my adviser and advocate, John Coyne; my friends David and Lynn Hassler
and Amy Stolls; my extraordinary colleagues in the English Department at West
Virginia University, especially Gail and Tim Adams, Jim Harms, Kevin Oderman, Katy
Ryan, and Ethel Morgan Smith; and my wife, Julie Penn, and my daughters, Annabel
and Rebecca Brazaitis, who are my light and devotion.

I am grateful to the editors of the journals in which the following stories
first appeared: "The Poet and the General" in Hayden's Ferry Review; "Before
the Wedding" in Shennandoah; "Air Conditioning and Heat" and "The Ferry" in
Permafrost; "The Life He Left Behind" in The Carolina Quarterly; "Defending The
Woman" (as "Defending Madonna") in Volt; "An American Affair" in North Dakota
Quarterly; "The Foreign Correspondent," in Confrontation; "The Race" in Whiskey
Island; and "Coming Home" in Baybury Review.

The writing of these stories was supported by a literature fellowship from
the National Endowment for the Arts and a Senate Research Grant and a Riggle
Fellowship from West Virginia University.

Library of Congress Cataloging-in-Publication Data

Brazaitis, Mark, 1966-
    An American affair : stories / Mark Brazaitis.-- 1st ed.
        p. cm.
    ISBN 1-881515-77-X (alk. paper)
    1. Latin America--Fiction. 2. Americans--Latin America--Fiction. I. Title.
PS3552.R3566A83 2005
813'.54--dc22

                                                    2005013634

For my mother, my sister, and Julie,
who nourish me, who make me laugh

Contents

An American Affair

The Poet and the General

For her interview with the General, the poet wears a black sweater and a black skirt. Her skirt falls past her knees, long enough to be modest. It is tight enough, however, to show off her hips and behind. Her sweater is loose enough to be modest. It is not too loose, however, to hide her breasts. She wears a touch of blush and a touch of lipstick and a generous amount of eye shadow to highlight her blue-gray eyes. She thinks it would enhance her profile of the General if, in keeping with his reputation, he tried to seduce her. She is twenty-six years old.

At her hotel in the capital, where in the late afternoon maids dried bed sheets by hanging them on ropes on the rooftop, she wrote down a line, anticipating her interview: *His hands, which have been used to punctuate orders of slaughter, touch my forearms, and I think of how fat his fingers are—the fingers of a fourth-grader whose mother puts too much butter on his bread.*

As an undergraduate at NYU, she majored in English literature and wrote her senior thesis on feminist refrains in Emily Dickinson's poetry. She minored in French. In graduate school in Iowa, she sat at the ends of long tables in poetry workshops. "But how," she often wondered of her classmates' well-crafted but mild work, "will it change the way anyone sees the world?"

Over the two years of her master's program, she produced a series of poems she called *New York Monologues*, written from the perspective of three dozen New Yorkers, from the mayor to the Chinese woman with pockmarked skin who sells batteries on the subway. She read the "Arts & Leisure" page of *The New York Times* every afternoon in the library, occasionally commenting to whoever was nearby about what off-Broadway show she would be seeing if she weren't holed up in the Midwest. To show her disdain for the self-absorbed, puerile men in her program, she dated a migrant worker from Mexico one autumn—all the Spanish she knows she learned during this time—although no one at the university seemed to care or even notice, and when one night he produced from his pocket a three-pack of condoms, as if the security of latex was what had stalled her from consummating their relationship, she said, in her mingled Spanish and English, "*Lo siento, pero* . . . this isn't working." His nostrils flared and something she didn't understand left his lips. Nevertheless, she has chosen to remember the relationship fondly.

The sun set an hour ago. At the General's residence—a general, she decides, cannot be said to live in a house—she waits in the dim hallway. It is less gaudy than she imagined. Where, she wonders, are the stuffed jaguars and tigers or at least the rifles mounted on the wall? The curtains, she notices, are red, and she takes comfort in this. She could have imagined red curtains. The coffee table in front of her holds the day's *El Gráfico* and an old fishing magazine from the States.

She is writing the profile for *The Progressive*, an alternative New York magazine for which she has written several pieces, including a 5,000-word feature entitled "A Day in the Life of Coney Island," which she opened with a mock monologue by the Cyclone, the roller coaster. The magazine promised to pay for her plane ticket, but only if she actually got an interview with the General. If she didn't, she was prepared to call her trip a working holiday. She plans during her stay to write a number of poems about the country and is hoping they'll be enough to make a chapbook. She has a tentative title: *Blood and Mangoes*.

Despite the invigorating tropical climate—hot during the day, cool and refreshing after sundown—the people she met in the United States Embassy all seemed to have the sad, gray faces of mourners. Gil Trumbell, the public affairs specialist, arranged her interview. "I won't lie," Trumbell said. "He'll see you only because you're pretty."

In her notebook, she wrote, *Even the Americans here acquiesce to the General's need for beautiful things. I am granted an interview because I am, to my mixed feelings of satisfaction and disgust, one of those things.*

The embassy man, Gil Trumbell, told the General the reporter was pretty. "You'll like her. She's your kind of woman."

The General smiled because he knew he was supposed to smile, a large, lecherous smile, and asked what he knew Gil Trumbell was expecting him to ask: "Blond?"

"Of course."

He agreed to the hour-long interview because to have refused the chance to entertain a blond *norteamericana*, no matter how insignificant her publication, would have been to add to the speculation he has seen written in ever less cautious lines in newspapers. This morning's *Prensa Libre,* reporting about the exhibit he'd opened at the Museo Nacional, said he "looked pale and seemed distracted, as if he hasn't slept."

Because only reporters from *El Gráfico* were permitted to attend the exhibit's opening, the General cannot be sure who was watching him and sharing their observations with *La Prensa.* Whoever it was, however, was right. For the last few nights, the General has slept no more than two hours at a time. It's his prostate, waking him like a small child's hand squeezing his bladder. He wonders what will kill him first, an assassin's bullet or his cancer. He knows the former would be a more merciful and dignified death, but if no assassin has stepped forward with a gun or grenade in the last five years, it's unlikely he will now. It isn't the act of dying he fears so much as what happens afterwards. He imagines sitting on the floor of a gray room with no windows and no doors.

He would like to meet the reporter in his hallway, sit with her in front of the coffee table and answer her questions quickly. Or he would like to say, "You know who I am—I am what everyone says—so write as if we've talked," and retreat to his bedroom, where, at ten o'clock, he watches *The Three Stooges* on Canal Cinco. The dubbing is bad, but his hearing isn't good anyway, and what he likes best about the three clowns they are able to convey without words. They may punch and poke each other, but theirs is the loving brutality of brothers. The General's own brother died when he was sixteen. He'd been playing soccer, and he chased a wayward ball into the street. A banana truck, coming down a hill from a nearby plantation, crushed him under its heavy wheels.

Francisco, his *muchacho*, comes to tell him the reporter is here. The General says, as he knows he is expected to say, "Escort her to my study." He hears her walk down the hallway with Francisco and distinguishes her footsteps above Francisco's tread. They clack with the innocent and urgent sense of purpose of two fingers on a typewriter.

Before stepping into his study, the General stops in front of a mirror in the hallway to adjust his collar and touch down a loose strand of his black hair. He would like to see himself as she will see him, as his country sees him, and he tries: he stands taller, he squares his shoulders, he puffs out his chest. It is no use—he sees his father as he was in the months before he died, after a stroke had wiped the magnificent sternness from his face. He hadn't wanted to look at his father, but he couldn't help seeing the way his father's mouth drooped on one side, exposing the yellowed bottoms of his teeth.

If I tell her I am dying, he thinks, she will, in her article, set my life against the thousands I have had murdered. She will write, "The General is dying, but because of his orders, he is in large company. If the afterlife is more just than this life, he will walk a corridor lined with the men, women, and children whose lives he shortened, and in the miles of his march toward hell, he will have to listen to their howls of glee and condemnation."

But what she wouldn't know is this: he would prefer their rancor, would welcome their scorn, over the silence of the gray room.

The General's handshake, as she expected, is firm, although his hands are smaller and more tender than she imagined. *His hands, which have been used to punctuate orders of slaughter, are the delicate hands of a fourteen-year-old who spends his days far from the ball field and tool shed.* He asks her what she wants to drink, and before she can reply, he suggests a glass of Argentinean wine "from the vineyards of my good friend, General Ramirez." His English is slow and precise and comforting. This is what she expected. If all Latin American leaders have such a voice, she can understand how Graham Greene could have loved Torrijos, how Gabriel García Márquez can love Castro.

But she cannot allow him to win this first exchange. She turns to Francisco, the stooped servant with white hair and salt-and-pepper mustache, and says, "*Un agua mineral, por favor.*" *I refuse his offer of wine, the wine his brother General sends in generous bottles from Argentina, and he counters my audacity, my resistance, with a smile.*

The General smiles before waving Francisco into the hallway. "You are," the General says, turning back to her, "a poet."

She is startled that he knows this, and she fears his knowledge of her poetry writing will detract from the image she wants to project of a tough journalist, a single-minded crusader against the evil over which he presides.

"Yes. How did you know?" *If he knows I write poetry, my one collection published by a university press and my single poems found only in literary magazines with circulations under five hundred, what must he know about his own people?*

"I have sources," the General says. Francisco returns with the drinks, and the General picks up the glass of *agua mineral* from Francisco's tray and hands it to her. He picks up his glass of red wine. "But this piece of information required no—how do you say—investigation. Mr. Trumbell told me. Cheers."

She is both relieved and disappointed. She will not be able to write about the eerie, inexplicable way the General knows her life. At the same time, she prefers to keep her history to herself.

"Sit down," he says, and she sits in a leather chair. He sits in its companion across from her. She places her glass of *agua mineral* on the coffee table between them and removes her tape recorder from her purse.

"Oh no," the General says. "I insist: No tape recorder."

"No?"

"Of course, I have nothing to hide." He is, she understands, being ironic. She can see this in his grin and the amused light in his eyes. "I prefer that you use no notes at all."

She wants to protest, although she suspects it would be futile. This is all right. She will use his refusal to her advantage. *The General wants no record of our conversation. He probably wishes the murders of thousands of his country's citizens could go equally unrecorded, a mere matter of opinion and suspect recollection.*

"As a schoolboy, I liked the poetry of Edgar Allan Poe," the General says. He takes a sip of his wine. "We were learning English, and the teacher—he was an American, born in Pittsburgh—used poetry to teach us." He pauses. "'Bells, bells, bells, bells, bells, bells, bells.'"

The General's mouth sags, and his strong, handsome features disappear, replaced by the worn, perplexed face of an old man. Her glimpse into what he will become makes her uncomfortable. She had expected to be confronted with a fixed visage, the ever stern and chiseled face she has seen painted on the sides of buildings in the capital.

"It was easy to remember this poem," he says, his face restored to its blank handsomeness. "Half the poem is 'bells.'"

"It's interesting you should quote from this poem," she says. "Why?"

"Because the last bells in the poem are funeral bells." She leans toward him, a calculated challenge. "And this country is known for its funerals."

"Oh," he says in a flat voice. "So we are beginning the interview." He drinks again from his wineglass. "You have come to ask me about our civil war."

"Some people think it's less than a civil war. Some people call it organized slaughter."

"In certain neighborhoods of your country, perhaps, they call it slaughter. It is easy to call it slaughter when you live on Park Avenue and read the liberal newspapers. But in my country, this is a war to preserve our rights and our freedoms. We have the right to own our own land. We have the right to own our own businesses. We are free men and women. If the rebels win, the state will own us."

He speaks in a strong, clear voice, as he might from a podium during a rally, but she notices how his eyes are focused above her shoulder, as if he is seeing something in the corner of the room. She is tempted to turn around, to see what he sees, but she doesn't want him to think she isn't listening.

"You are called the Butcher of Bananera."

He looks at her and produces a smile. Again, he is as she imagined: suave and commanding. "This is a nickname my enemies have given me. My grandchildren have also given me a nickname: *Papá Pacífico*. Gentle father. I believe they are in a better position to know the truth."

She knows he is lying. Perhaps he even knows she knows. *He is the country's chief of lies, of disinformation, and he thinks nothing of inventing a lie on the spot about his grandchildren. Clever how they, like Poe, speak in alliteration.*

"You are continuing a relentless campaign, burning down villages you suspect are sympathetic to the guerrillas. But international observers have estimated the number of guerrillas to be fewer than one thousand. Certainly they don't represent much of a threat anymore."

"Wherever there is someone who wants to destroy the rights and freedoms we have, we are threatened. But about the villages, I think you have false information. The fires that have destroyed villages have been set by the villagers themselves. They have found enemies in their communities, and they have set fire to their enemies' houses. Some of the fires, unfortunately, have spread out of control."

"General, do you expect me—or anyone—to believe this?" He isn't looking at her again. This time, she does glance behind her, but there is nothing in the corner save the meeting of two walls. When she looks at him again, he smiles, but his smile is more tired than a General's smile should be at eight-thirty on a Thursday night. She is tempted to ask him if he's all right, but the question seems inappropriate—and far from anything she'd ever expected to ask.

She begins to ask her question again when he interrupts: "You haven't been a good drinking partner. Look." He points to her *agua mineral.* "It is half full. And I have already finished my wine. At this rate—and given what each of us is drinking—I will become drunk much more quickly than you. But perhaps this is an old journalistic technique, no?"

He laughs, and she decides his seduction of her has begun. *Failing to interest me in his Argentinean wine, he tries another strategy: charm. Even though I know what it is and toward what end it hopes to speed, I am half lulled by its cadences.*

"When I was studying in the United States, at Harvard, I used to go drinking with members of the soccer team." The General's connection to Harvard—he studied for a year at the Kennedy School of Government—has caused the university some embarrassment. "I missed the soccer of my country, so I was a fan of the team, and the players rewarded me by buying me beer. Sometimes they asked me to sing songs from my country and I obliged, even if my voice was—how shall I say—like a canary with flu." He pauses and looks past her. "Yes, I loved to watch soccer."

The General sighs the last word like the name of an old girl-friend, and, for a moment, she is carried by his wistfulness. Her high school boyfriend used to play soccer.

The General is looking at her with a certain hopefulness, like a man in a bar wanting to tell a story, but she refuses to pursue this part of his past. He is no sentimental, middle-aged man, doomed to consider his year at Harvard, when he was forty-two and a handsome but undistinguished army captain, the best of his life. He is the Butcher of Bananera. Nevertheless, she has been tripped up in her sense of who he is. She knew him better before she stepped into his residence.

"Are you telling me the people in the villages started the fires?"

"I was telling you about soccer."

The General would rather talk about soccer. No, he would rather not talk at all. He would prefer to be in his bed, waiting until ten when he will turn on his television and watch *The Three Stooges*.

She believes I am a murderer, he thinks. And I am. But I always believed in what I was doing.

He always believed until the slow drip of his urine at night became unbearable and the doctor, with a diploma from Duke University on his office wall, told him he had cancer. This happened two weeks ago, and the doctor recommended vigorous treatment because the cancer was advanced. "General, you are only fifty-six years old. You have a chance to beat the cancer. But you will need treatment in the United States."

Was it at this moment that he'd thought of the dead? No, it was later. He'd left the doctor's office, and instead of having Francisco drive him back home, he'd elected to walk. It was dangerous to walk alone on the streets of the capital without an armed escort, but the doctor's revelation made him feel reckless. He'd been introduced not to Death—as a soldier, he knew Death, he'd killed men, he'd seen his fellow soldiers die in front of him—but his own death, and this was something different.

As he walked unrecognized past men with wooden pushcarts of ice cream standing in the shade of bougainvillea and women selling roses in the middle of intersections, he thought of the people killed because of the war—people he'd ordered killed and people killed in his name or the name of the cause. He felt precisely what they'd lost. It was late afternoon, and the sun cast a rose-colored glow over the hoods of cars and the leaves of avocado trees, and he was grateful and satisfied to be seeing this small piece of everyday miracle.

The real enemy, he thought, as a woman approached him with her roses, a woman with blackened teeth and a scar above her left eyebrow, was Death. The real enemy was Death, and the woman was beautiful, beautiful because she was alive. If he'd had his wallet—it was with Francisco in the car, which followed him at a crawl—he would have bought all her flowers.

"General?"

"Yes?"

"You haven't answered my question."

He produces a smile, although he doesn't know what purpose it is supposed to serve. He has forgotten her question; it must be obvious. He planned this interview to be different—he planned to be everything she expected. But now, again, over her shoulder, he sees his father and brother. They are standing side by side as if on a soccer field, a pair of defenders awaiting a penalty kick.

"I think, perhaps, it's time to talk of something else besides the war," he says. "It's clear you and I disagree on what the war means. You will write what you believe, and I and my people will continue to fight for what we believe. Fortunately, your government is a little more sympathetic to our cause than you are."

His remark stalls her as she searches for another question or another way to ask the same question. She is, as Gil Trumbell said, attractive, but if in his younger days he would have been drawn to what is most American about her—her blond hair, her blue eyes, her ample breasts pressed against her black sweater—he finds himself gazing at her ears.

Before they were married, when they were both teenagers, the General and his wife used to escape to the banana fields behind the high school, and in the shade of banana trees, she'd pull her long, black hair behind her head. In their embrace, between kisses, he'd call her, half teasingly, half affectionately, "Princess Little Ears." He hasn't seen his wife in three months. She lives with their sons and their sons' families behind a three-meter, barbed wire fence in their mansion in Bananera.

"The latest military aid from the United States," she says, "comes with a few qualifications. You have to conform with specific human rights requirements, including withdrawing your army from fourteen villages in the north with a majority Indian population. Do you think you'll be able to meet these standards?"

"We are always happy to work with the United States. We respect the United States. And we are positive we can show your government our compliance with human rights. But if the United

States fails to be persuaded, if, in other words, our enemies are successful in their campaign of lies and disinformation, we will continue our campaign. Our victory is inevitable, with or without help."

This, he believes, is true. The war's outcome has been inevitable from the beginning, but only recently has he accepted this. When, five years ago, he came to power after overthrowing General Carpio, he believed what others told him: he was the man to end forever guerrilla and Indian designs on revolution. He ordered more soldiers into the jungles of the north and into the mangrove swamps of the south. He ordered more Indians to be impressed into the army, knowing if Indian soldiers fought Indian guerrillas, the army's cause would be furthered no matter who was killed. An Indian dead is an Indian dead, no matter what uniform he is wearing. All this seemed like his idea, but he discovered he had only proposed what had been suggested months and even years before by the men who'd occupied this same presidential house on the outskirts of the capital. And, as always, the army was successful in the north and less successful in the south. And the number of guerrillas, as always, continued to dwindle.

Meanwhile, an editorialist from the underground *La Hora* dubbed him "The Butcher of Bananera" and the nickname rippled across the country, whispered in corn fields and town squares. In ever larger numbers, guerrillas fled their cave hideouts in the mountains and jungles and spilled into neighboring countries with stories of atrocities—decapitations, burnings, rapes—speaking of them as if he, the General, had invented them, as if they were a new horror he'd introduced into the three-decades-long war, as if they knew nothing of the Spanish Conquest or Napoleon or their supposed heroes, Lenin and Stalin.

"When will you order the troops to withdraw from the fourteen Indian villages?"

"They will be leaving soon."

They have, in fact, left. Nine of the villages have been burned to the ground. In the other five, men between the ages of fourteen and thirty-five have either been killed or impressed into the army. The General ordered three of the villages burned, but this had already been done before his order was received. The rest of the burnings and murders and forced recruitments occurred in the random course of the war—on lieutenants' orders or soldiers' own initiatives.

If at first the General was reluctant to acknowledge the discrepancy between what he imagined his power would be and what it actually was, he accepts it now. This life, however short it falls of how he once envisioned it, nevertheless brings him this house, Francisco, his bed, his television. He won't leave it voluntarily, even to fight his cancer. To go to the United States for the prolonged treatment he requires would mean surrendering all he presides over, and he has become possessive of it, as one becomes possessive of a woman.

He suspects he would even miss his occasional visitors who, like this blond-haired, blue-eyed poet, sit in his study in order to confirm what they already think of him. He is, of course, their accomplice, even tonight, when he is tired and therefore in more danger of revealing, by a careless word or gesture, some thought or emotion he must keep to himself. If it's truth the poet wants, she would have better luck interrogating his father and brother, whose silence from the corner of the room is the most sincere answer of the night.

"General, do you ever have trouble sleeping?"

"I sleep," he replies, smiling, "like the dead."

Francisco has brought her another *agua mineral*, even though she hasn't finished the first. "You must tell me," the General says, "about your poetry."

"I am here to interview you."

"Yes, and you have interviewed me. But it is only fair you tell me a little about yourself."

"There isn't much to tell."

"I'm sure there is. When did you start writing poetry?"

"When I was ten years old."

"Why did you write?"

Her father loved poetry. He was a lawyer who would rather have been an English professor, and his library, a dark corner room in an otherwise bright house, was full of leather volumes of Coleridge, Wordsworth, Shelley and Byron. He himself wrote poetry on occasion, and one summer, when he was in his twenties, he attended the Bread Loaf Writers' Conference, where he heard Robert Frost read. He returned home with a signed copy of Frost's *A Witness Tree*, which, over the course of his life, he seemed to prize more than anything he owned.

Was it her father's esteem she was seeking when she started writing poetry? Yes, but it was more than this.

"I wanted to give meaning to my experiences—and to other people's."

With her words, she could bring back to life scenes and sounds from her past and give them shape and coherence. Eventually, it wasn't only her own life about which she felt inspired to write. Writing poetry gave her permission to inhabit other people's bodies and minds, to imagine what they saw and felt. Exercising her creativity forced her to be more compassionate. With pen in hand, she tried to understand what other people endured.

"And have you succeeded?"

"I don't know," she replies. "I don't think I'm in the best position to judge."

"I would like to hear one of your poems," the General says.

"I don't know them by heart." This isn't true, but she doesn't want the conversation focused on her. This isn't why she's here.

"So you will deny me this pleasure?"

She watches the General's eyes. If this is part of his attempt to flatter her, to charm her, to seduce her, it isn't working. He seems to know it wouldn't because as soon as he finishes the exchange, he again stares over her shoulder. He has, it seems, fulfilled an obligation, no matter how half-hearted, although what the obligation might be, she doesn't know. She is, however, tempted to do what he has requested, if only because she feels slighted by his apparent indifference.

But on second thought, she wonders if his indifference is calculated to inspire this very response from her. In being detached, isn't he drawing her to him in a way she wouldn't be if he were looking at her with intense, curious eyes?

But as she reflects again, she wonders if she is over reflecting. Again, she feels unsure of the man sitting in front of her. Her profile of him is unwriting itself. Having been complete before she arrived, it is losing lines each minute she sits with him. At the end of the night, she fears, she will be left with nothing. But perhaps this is the place to start: the General is nothing.

No, she thinks, he is the Butcher of Bananera. He can't be nothing. Nothing doesn't cause the misery he has caused.

"Do you read poetry now, General?"

"Sometimes."

"And you don't see a contradiction between reading poetry and . . . "

"And presiding over a civil war? Abraham Lincoln did the same."

"But Abraham Lincoln . . . "

"What? Didn't order the burning of villages? Are you forgetting Sherman's march to the sea? And Abraham Lincoln didn't have people slaughtered? Ulysses Grant was the original 'Butcher.' Their very barbarity is why Lincoln liked these generals—and why they were successful. And all three men are considered heroes in your country."

Despite his clever arguments, the General seems disengaged from the conversation. He is employing lines he might have used in his Harvard days. She thinks: he doesn't believe anything he's saying. Then she thinks he believes everything he's saying, and because he believes it, because he has always believed it, he doesn't need to say it with particular conviction.

"Do you consider yourself a hero, General?"

In the profile she would have written before she arrived at the General's residence, his answer would have been: "If I am a hero, it is only because our cause is heroic." And she would have written: *The General is obviously satisfied with his answer, because he sits back in his chair and strokes his chin contentedly. He thinks he has managed to be self-deprecating in his response, but he has only deepened his aura of pomposity and megalomania.*

Now she doesn't know how he will answer. And he doesn't satisfy her curiosity. He doesn't answer at all. Instead, he stands up. "It's late. And because it's late—and because the streets of our capital are, one might say, unpredictable at this hour—I will provide you with an armed escort back to your hotel."

Although he appears unhurried, she wonders if he has another appointment after her. Perhaps he has a mistress waiting for him. Perhaps he wants to confer with an advisor.

"No, thank you, General," she says. "I'll take a taxi."

"Very well," he says. "As you wish."

She cannot resist a last question: "What will you do now, General?"

"Now?" he asks. "This minute?"

"Yes."

"I will go to sleep, of course." He smiles. "Do you believe me?"

She doesn't. His life can't be this simple. She knows it isn't. "No," she says.

He pauses a moment before laughing. "You're right."

She sits on the rooftop of her hotel, her notebook in her lap. She wants to write down everything about her conversation with the General before she forgets it. But she is distracted by the pair of sheets, still hanging on the ropes strung between poles. Flap, flap, flap. Their sound is like the beating of wings, although it's a futile beating. They will never fly.

I've been tricked, she thinks. Played with. Deceived. But I don't know how.

The General's last words come back to her: "You're right." He was going to do something after she left, and whatever it was, she thinks, holds the key to his brutality, his evil. And whatever it was, she can't envision it. For once, her imagination fails her; as potent as it has seemed to her, it retreats in the face of the General's depravity and inscrutability.

She hates him because he has eluded her. She hates him because she can't hate him in the way she'd like to hate him.

She tries to write down their conversation, but she finds she can barely remember it. She tries to begin from the line she wrote down in the morning: *His hands, which have been used to punctuate orders of slaughter . . . .* She stops. What she finds herself writing next are lines from an Emily Dickinson poem. She didn't include this poem in her college study of Dickinson's feminism, but, rather, remembers it from her childhood. Her father liked to read it to her, and it comforted her because it made the world seem silly and harmless.

Now, however, as she looks out across the capital city, at the gray outlines of volcanoes and mountains in the distance, she is reminded of the countless dead in this country she is only visiting, and the poem seems to be written in their voices, with a sad authority she could never reproduce in any profile she might write about the General or in any poem she might write about the world she has discovered here:

I'm Nobody! Who are you?
Are you—Nobody—Too?

There is only one minute to go, and the General tries to

savor the pleasure of his anticipation. He breathes deeply and feels the blood pulse throughout his body—in his forearms and in his neck and in his cancerous groin. Tonight, he is alive, and as he sits in his bed, the fresh white sheet, smelling of the lemon soap the maid uses, pulled across his chest, he smells life's pleasure, feels life's pulse. In two or three hours, when he is asleep, his bladder will bother him and he'll stumble toward the bathroom, and as he is urinating in the dark, he'll think of his death and be afraid. But now he is, again, reconciled to life, gleeful with anticipation at its promise.

And here comes the carnival music, and a moment later, they appear—Larry, Curly, Moe—dancing, stumbling, across his television screen. He is laughing even before they've said a word.

She has heard the song probably two dozen times in the last week, and she hears it again when she turns on the radio in her kitchen. She can't sleep. Her fiancé is in the bedroom. She has left him in order to sit and stare at her face in the window and listen on low volume to whatever music she can find on the radio at this late hour. It's the same song, the one with her name in it, the chorus the only part she understands:

> *Elena!*
> *Elena!*
> *Estoy loco por tu amor.*

After five years in Guatemala, she speaks Spanish well and only occasionally has trouble with the language, standing dumbfounded in the market after a tomato vendor makes a joke or, when she's tired and not paying attention, nodding ignorantly to words her fiancé has spoken. But she can't understand what the singer of the song with her name in it is saying in the verses, can't hold on to a single word. True, his pronunciation is terrible. Nevertheless, she knows she should be able to understand at least some of it.

> *Elena!*
> *Elena!*
> *Estoy loco por tu amor.*

Her name isn't Elena, but Helen. She adopted the name Elena because it's the Spanish equivalent of hers. She's been known as Elena ever since she came to Guatemala as a Peace Corps volunteer. Even Flavio, her fiancé, calls her Elena.

She *is* Elena. Helen was someone who lived in a three-bedroom apartment on the East Side of Manhattan with Peter. They were both lawyers, working sixty-hour weeks and making enough money to talk about hiring a nanny for their future child. They planned to marry in May. In April, she called the 150 people to whom they'd sent invitations and told them there wouldn't be a wedding. In September, she was on an airplane to Guatemala.

Now she is about to marry Flavio Morales, a man worlds different from her ex-fiancé. But like the first time, she can't sleep. She's thirty-three years old, too old to be repeating what she did when she was twenty-six. There were no invitations to the wedding this time, only word of mouth. The Catholic Church in Cobán, the large town to the north, is reserved for Saturday and will be full.

Elena!
Elena!
Estoy loco por tu amor.

The song is ending, and she's glad. It disturbs her, gnaws at her unease, makes her feel like she did when she first came to Guatemala, speaking only the barest Spanish and understanding less. She wants to yell at the singer to enunciate, but he is gone and another song plays.

Turning off the radio, she stares at her reflection in the window. It's a poor reflection. If she didn't know who she was looking at, she wouldn't be able to tell if it was man or a woman, someone beautiful or ugly. If she could see herself, she thinks, she would see her unease reflected in the droop of her jaw and the light blue ovals under her eyes. She used to be pretty, with light-blond hair and pale skin that, nevertheless, tanned instead of burned. Now her skin is always tan, with a tint of red she sees as an augury of melanoma. She works all day in the sun. After finishing her Peace Corps tour, she stayed in Guatemala to run an organic farm and training center with Flavio. She loves the work. She thinks she loves the man.

The next morning, Flavio is turning the compost heap in the middle of the field. Elena approaches him carefully, to observe him without him being aware of it. She sees him: straight black hair, left a little long for her benefit; thin arms which nevertheless have significant muscles, the result of working long hours outdoors; thick legs over boots half buried in soil. In the midst of their wedding preparations, Elena and Flavio are also planning to host a group of *técnicos* from Guatemala's ministry of agriculture. It's a three-day course, scheduled to begin the day after the wedding. When the course is over, they will spend their honeymoon on the island of Roatan off the coast of Honduras.

As Elena comes closer to her fiancé, she discovers he is whistling, and she recognizes the song as the one she keeps hearing on the radio. She wants to ask him what the lyrics mean, but when she calls his name he stops whistling and looks at her with concern. In his low, controlled voice, he says, "You haven't been sleeping well."

She admits this is true, and points to the blue ovals under her eyes as confirmation. He asks why, and she tells him it's natural to be nervous before her wedding. He moves more compost with his shovel. He's wearing a T-shirt she gave him before they were lovers. The front of the T-shirt is emblazoned with the name of a now-defunct rock group whose concert in Madison Square Garden she attended with Peter.

"Are you nervous?" she asks.

He stops shoveling to stare at her and smile. He has nice white teeth, free of the gaudy fillings she sees on many Guatemalans. "I'm not nervous," he says. "I've never slept like I do now, so peacefully."

She guesses he is trying to reassure her, as if his own confidence in what they are about to do will ease her doubts. But it only angers her. Of course he can sleep, she thinks. He's marrying a *gringa*, a blond *gringa*. All his friends envy him, even the smart ones, his classmates from the university who should be able to see the drawbacks to such a marriage. Flavio won't get to be a typical Guatemalan husband. He'll have to put up with her independence, in whatever form it takes. She'll be able to visit other men, alone. She'll keep her own bank account. She'll keep her name. She wonders if perhaps he doesn't understand this, if he thinks, deep down, that once they're married, she'll be magically converted, by wedding gown and vow, into a Guatemalan wife.

"I'm glad one of us is sleeping well," she says, trying to put something ironic and spiteful in her inflection, but it doesn't work. It rarely does. He takes her comment at face value, smiles and continues to shovel.

She misses the subtleties that come with speaking her own language. If she wants to be understood in Spanish, she has to be direct. At first, she liked this forced honesty; she'd had to abandon the masks she used to wear and enhance with ambiguous phrases. It's hard to lie in a foreign language.

Now she wishes again for nuance. She knows Spanish is full of fine distinctions, but she has come to the language too late to be fluent in its grace and flexibility. This troubles her.

She tells Flavio she's going to attempt to sleep and she'll come help him later, when he's weeding the corn field. The corn field is their joy. They've used only natural fertilizers and pesticides, including a concoction Flavio improvised from garlic, coffee, and soap, and they are looking forward to showing it to the representatives from the agricultural ministry.

As she is walking back to the house, she turns to look again at Flavio. She is surprised to see him gazing at her, with a look both wistful and worried. Now it is she who smiles to reassure him. She has saved one of her masks after all.

Inside the house, she fixes a cup of coffee and sits at the kitchen table, which she and Flavio made when they moved in together. Most of what is in their house they either made or bought together. She'd wanted as many links between them as possible. It seemed important. She had been surprised at how easy it had been to separate from Peter. They had each brought a certain number of household items to the relationship, and when the relationship ended, there was no argument over who owned what. The painless division of goods made Elena wonder how connected they'd ever been. If she were to break up with Flavio, the distribution of property would be a messy matter. She finds comfort in this.

She thinks about turning on the radio but doesn't want to hear the song with her name in it. She wants to let her mind ride a caffeine buzz to wherever it might take her. A moment later, however, she hears someone tapping on the door. It's María, who lives in a small house across the field with her two children. To feed them, she raises chickens and pigs and sometimes does her neighbors' laundry. She is probably close to thirty, but looks older, with sagging breasts and crow's feet.

Elena doesn't feel like talking, but she doesn't have the energy to think up an excuse to turn María away, so she opens the door and invites her inside. She brings María a cup of coffee and they both sit drinking a while before María speaks: "Are you ready for the wedding?"

"Yes," Elena says, then adds, "and no."

María looks at her curiously, and Elena knows she will have to elaborate. She could, she thinks, answer on a practical level, describing which wedding preparations have been completed and which haven't, but she is too tired to catalogue every item. Besides, Flavio's sister is in charge of the wedding's practical details, and Elena doesn't know how much she has left to do. Sighing, she prepares to tell María the truth and is relieved that she has made this decision. It will be hard to convey her ambiguity in Spanish, although she hopes speech will help end it.

She decides to start with Peter and their apartment on East 87th Street, about as distant from the countryside of Guatemala as it's possible to imagine. She envisions María, in her loose *güipil* and faded *corte*, walking down Park Avenue with her barefoot children following. The image makes her smile.

She describes her life with Peter, their busy schedules and future plans. "There was something about the life I didn't like. It wasn't really Peter I didn't like." She stops, sips her coffee. The caffeine helps, but, tired, she is having trouble expressing herself. "I think it was me I didn't like. It was me living that life, working long hours, being part of that crazy lifestyle. I didn't have any time to know who I was. I was just what was all around me."

She isn't denied the opportunity to look inward now. The wide spaces and quiet nights in Guatemala have given her ample time to explore her soul. She has spent months ruminating, although this hasn't brought her much closer to an understanding of herself. What she has found inside her is an appetite for living she hasn't satisfied and doesn't know how to satisfy.

"I love Flavio," she tells María. "But I am worried I will not be happy in a few years." This isn't quite true. She is worried she won't be happy tomorrow. She is worried she isn't happy now.

María is married but hasn't seen her husband in two years. He took a job in the Petén, working on a road construction project with a company from England. María thinks he is still working on the project, although Elena knows it's long over.

"I was very scared before my wedding," María says. "I cried to my mother. Her *güipil* was wet when I finished. I didn't know my husband well. My father knew him and said he would be a good husband." María shakes her head. "My mother says my father is a good husband but not a good judge of other men."

Elena has no doubt that Flavio will be a good husband by María's standards, probably by most people's standards. She wonders, though, what her standards are and if Flavio will fulfill them. She has tried to imagine her life five years from now, has pictured children and an ever-expanding organic farm with more and more technical groups coming for seminars, not only from Guatemala but other Latin American countries and perhaps even the States. She has tried to image Flavio helping her raise the children and lead the seminars. They are a good team now, and Elena thinks they could be a good team for a long time if she can only satisfy herself that this is the life she wants.

María looks at her sadly, and Elena realizes there has been a long pause in their conversation. She doesn't know quite how to break the silence, so she asks María if she's happy. She uses the verb *ser,* to mean a permanent happiness, but María must assume Elena has made a mistake because she answers by saying she is happy having coffee and talking with Elena.

"But in general," Elena says. "Are you happy in general?"

María considers, frowns. "It is hard sometimes," she says. She smiles. "Yes?" Then she shakes her head. "I don't know."

"I don't know either," Elena says.

Despite the inconclusiveness of what they've shared, Elena feels heartened by her conversation with María. It is the same feeling of casual wonder she experiences when she and Flavio exchange ideas about compost, a crop, the evils of cattle ranching. Elena always finds something remarkable about being able to leap through language and culture and reach him, though she has long told herself it isn't remarkable at all since they've always been more similar than different. All his adult life, Flavio has been a vegetarian. And one night, before they were dating, he spoke to her over tea at El Tirol, a café in Cobán, about the oppression of women in his country. She could have given a similar speech about women in the United States.

Peter, too, had considered himself a liberal, but his beliefs had few manifestations in his life. Growing up, he attended private schools, and he used to spend summers with his parents in the Hamptons. Although he talked righteously about civil rights, the only meaningful contact he'd had with blacks was with the woman from Jamaica who cleaned his parents' apartment and called him "Mister Peter." Occasionally they talked dreamily of starting a law firm that would specialize in the rights of indigents, but it was easier to send a check every few months to the Coalition for the Homeless. Probably wrongly, she blamed Peter for their life of all talk and no action.

In contrast, Flavio signed on as an agronomist with the Guatemalan government after graduating from college. He and Elena had worked together when she was a Peace Corps volunteer, and she followed him into mountains, where he taught farmers how to build drainage ditches and plant lemon grass to stop the soil from eroding. He'd introduced them to compost piles and natural pesticides, cheap alternatives to the chemicals they couldn't afford but were buying anyway.

As a girl in Ohio, Elena had lived on her grandparents' farm, and she knew about the care of chickens and pigs, areas with which Flavio wasn't as familiar. If a farmer needed his animals vaccinated, she was the one to do it. After they were engaged, they'd established the organic farm, and though Flavio continued to work for the government, he planned to quit when they were sure they could support themselves off the agricultural groups they hosted and the food they produced.

If there was one area where they didn't mesh from the beginning, it was lovemaking. Frustrated with Flavio's inexperienced groping, she tried to tell him how to please her. Her instructions tested her Spanish, which, in this case, proved halting and inept. One night, stuck without the right words, she found herself giggling, a reaction which offended Flavio's machismo. He stomped out of their bedroom, the only time she has ever seen him angry, and didn't return until dawn. Before long, she learned it was easier to lead him, letting her hands do the teaching.

Flavio is a good lover now, better than Peter ever was. Peter used to ask her if she wanted to make love, as if petitioning a judge to approach the bench, and while she was grateful for his consideration, she found it, after a while, tedious, and refused many nights with excuses increasingly less imaginative. Flavio does not use words to ask, but reads her response to his caresses. Half the time, it is she who inquires with her fingers and lips, no matter how redolent he is of the day's work. Sometimes they both stink, and this delights her, as much for the sense of triumph it gives her over her old life as for its own pungent pleasures.

She sees that María is looking at her again with concern, and Elena realizes she again has abandoned the conversation. She is about to apologize when she hears someone tapping on the screen door. She and María turn to see Cruz, María's six-year old daughter, barefoot and holding Marco, María's two-year-old son, who is sobbing. "*Con permiso*," María says, and although it can't be any fun to calm a screaming child, Elena imagines María is happy to escape the lagging conversation.

A few minutes later, Elena goes outside. The sun is bright without being hot, and she can hear birds singing and cows mooing, stronger sounds than the distant hum of bus engines. She walks toward the corn field and finds Flavio, his back turned to her, standing in the first row, using a hoe to skim the weeds. Behind him is a mountain, with a broken cloud above it. The mountain is beautiful. The cloud, even in pieces, is beautiful. Elena is relieved to have this beauty. This is what she wants.

With two days left before the wedding, Elena is again unable to sleep. She sits in the kitchen, listening on low volume to music she doesn't like. She is tired of thinking, worrying, spinning her life around inside her. She knows she'll feel better once she makes a decision, whether it's to marry Flavio or tell him she can't. If she rejects Flavio, she won't stay in Guatemala, but she hasn't thought where to go. This, she thinks, is significant. Before, she had a plan: she had applied to the Peace Corps six months before she broke up with Peter.

When Flavio comes into the kitchen, it takes her a few seconds to see him, so accustomed has she become to having this space, at night, to herself. He says nothing, but stands as if waiting for her to tell him something. She knows this is her opportunity to back out of the wedding, and she sees it wouldn't be difficult. Her sleepless nights, she realizes, have troubled him more than he's shown, and given him warning. He knows what happened with Peter.

"Hello" is all she can think to say, and he returns the greeting. He doesn't move any closer and she doesn't invite him to, but there is, oddly, little tension in the room. It's as if they've both decided something and are only waiting to confirm it.

She is grateful he has come and grateful he stopped where he did. Peter would have placed his hands on her shoulders, gripping too tightly, and spoken too quickly and too much, presuming to know what she was thinking. But Flavio is waiting for her words, and she obliges him: "I don't know who I am." These are the same words she said to Peter a few days before she told him she couldn't marry him. He had responded by saying that *he* knew who she was, even if she didn't, and he recited a list—lawyer, lover, softball player, rooftop gardener—each modified with adjectives like great and wonderful and superb, a litany of hyperbole. She didn't know what kind of response she'd wanted from Peter, but this hadn't been it.

Flavio, however, says nothing, and they listen to crickets chirping and the distant but distinct sounds of a cow complaining. "I wonder," he says softly, "if the crickets know who they are. I wonder if the cows know who they are."

This strikes Elena as something she might ponder and, before long, appreciate. Now, though, she is too intent on pushing toward a conclusion, on scaring him, if she can. She says, "Do you know who you are?"

He responds quickly, lightly: "I know I'm not a cricket or a cow."

She is tempted to laugh, to fall into the light familiarity they share, and forget, for now, her worries. In Guatemala, this is how even tragedy is skirted: with a wink, an aside, a joke. Something holds her back, however, and she remains stiff in her chair.

No doubt sensing her resolve, Flavio takes a seat beside her and shifts his body a few times to get comfortable, as if preparing for a prolonged stay. After a long silence, he says, "In Nicaragua, there was a famous baseball player, a catcher. He had a great natural talent and everyone loved him. With his strong arm, he could throw out any base runner. They called this catcher 'The Flamethrower.'"

Elena smiles tentatively, not sure why Flavio is talking about baseball. But his deep, calm voice is reassuring, like her grandfather's had been. Her grandfather was a baseball fan, and he used to listen to Indians games on the radio long after the invention of television. During her last year in her grandparents' house, the summer before she left for college, she used to come home late from her job at Kroger and find her grandfather sleeping in his chair, the radio playing on the table beside him. Inevitably he would wake up and ask, "What's the score?"

"One day, the Flamethrower discovered he couldn't get the

ball back to the pitcher," Flavio says. "He would toss the ball into the grass in front of the pitcher's mound or throw the ball three feet over the pitcher's head. The more he tried, the worse he became. If he wanted to get the ball to the pitcher, he had to walk it to him."

"What was wrong with him?" Elena asks.

Flavio shrugs. "People said he was thinking too much. He was thinking about throwing the ball instead of throwing it."

Elena is used to sports metaphors, having heard plenty from her grandfather, but she doesn't know how Flavio's is relevant. Nevertheless, she feels oddly comforted by it, and she doesn't ask out of animosity but only curiosity, "Why are you telling me this?"

Flavio shakes his head. "I don't know. I was thinking about it today when I was turning the compost pile. I wondered if by thinking about turning a compost pile, I wouldn't be able to." A pause. "But even after I thought about it, I could do it."

She laughs lightly, and Flavio, in apparent relief, allows himself a half smile. Deciding to put off agonizing until tomorrow, she stands, ready to come to him, to go back to bed, but she hears the song come on the radio, the song with her name in it. She stops, her doubts recalled. She suddenly considers it possible that she's not only with the wrong man but in the wrong place.

"Flavio," she says, her voice heavy with seriousness, "what is he singing?"

"He's singing, 'Elena, Elena, I'm crazy for your love.'"

"No," she says, her voice higher now and hinting at panic, "the verses. What do the verses say?"

Flavio looks at her, looks at the radio. His forehead wrinkles. "I don't know," he says. "I think the verses are in Portuguese. The chorus is in Spanish, but the verses are in Portuguese. The group must be from Brazil."

She feels as if she has found something she'd feared was lost or has returned to a familiar road after hours driving down nameless back streets. Her relief is nearly joy, and she celebrates by hugging Flavio and kissing him on the cheek a half dozen times, loud smacks. Even Flavio is surprised—she can feel it in his stiffness—but he soon relaxes, soon returns the kisses, although slower, the way she likes them. Wrapped around each other, they stumble to their bedroom and fall into the bed they made one afternoon, their hands blistered when they were finished, their bodies exhausted and yearning to celebrate their creation with sleep and love.

Air Conditioning and Heat

Walter Anderson's son steps into the airport bar wearing his
perpetual grin, the grin of someone who has unexpectedly but
not undeservedly found something delicious—a pear, a plum,
a chocolate Easter egg—at his feet. Andy is long-haired, long-
eared and long-faced. He has never been attractive—even as a
baby he was disproportionate, un-cutely oblong—but this has
never stopped him from being happy. To his father's enduring
puzzlement, he has always been carelessly, obliviously full of joy.

"Dad!" Andy spots his father at a table in a corner of the
Brew Pub in the Newark Airport. Behind Andy is a woman with
square shoulders and black hair. She isn't short or dark-skinned,
and Walter is forced to revise the image he had of her. When
Andy called to tell him he had married a Guatemalan woman,
he pictured the plump, sad-eyed girl who cleaned the tables of
the cantina in Tijuana where, when he was in the army three
decades ago, he used to spend an occasional Saturday night.

"Dad, hello." Andy opens his arms and gives his father as
much of a hug as Walter will permit. "This is Gloria."

"I am pleased to meet you," Gloria says, giggling and turning
to Andy, who says, "You said it perfectly."

"Nice to meet you, too," Walter says. "Sit down."

After they've settled into plastic seats, Walter says to his son,
"It's too bad you couldn't have come to Cleveland for a day or
two."

"I told you, Dad, the round-trip from Newark would have
cost us more than our flight to Spain."

"I would have been happy to pay for your ticket." Walter
glances at Gloria. "Both of your tickets."

"I know, and I appreciate it." Andy looks away, hiding, Walter suspects, a frown. He wonders if his son is thinking about whom he might have seen in Cleveland—about Rebecca, his former fiancée.

When Andy again looks at Walter, his oversized smile has returned. Walter has seen similar smiles on the drug company representatives who come to his office to talk up the latest pill or cream, but there is always a mercenary reason for their grins, their manufactured enthusiasm intended to sway him to their products.

Gloria whispers something to Andy, who laughs and tells Walter, "She says I don't look anything like you."

"Ask her if she thinks that's a good thing."

When Gloria gives Andy her answer, he scolds her in mock gruffness. "She says you're far better looking." Andy laughs so quickly and loudly that Walter, though flattered, doesn't feel the need to respond with anything but a forced smile.

To Gloria, Walter says, "I'm sorry you won't get to see the house where Andy grew up."

"Hell, Dad, she won't even get to see New York City. If we had more time, we could take a bus into town and walk around Times Square." Andy looks at his watch. "And speaking of time, our flight boards in forty minutes."

"I thought we had two hours."

"There was a schedule change."

"Jesus, Andy, I hoped we could talk. It's been a long time since we've even spoken on the phone."

"You'll have to come to see us in Guatemala."

"So you do plan to stay in Guatemala?" Walter asks his son.

"Yup."

"And what, exactly, will you do again—work on a cattle ranch?"

"Gloria's dad owns it. I'll learn how he runs his business. Maybe I'll start a business of my own one day."

Walter releases a large, involuntary sigh. "So when you told me what you planned to do after you finished the Peace Corps— go to law school or medical school—you weren't serious."

"I *was* serious. At the time." Andy lifts his shoulders in a quick, dismissive shrug. "A lot changed, obviously."

"I don't understand." This isn't rare. Walter has never understood his son. From an early age, Walter plied his son with balls—baseballs and tennis balls and basketballs—but Andy never liked any of the sports Walter liked, never liked any sports at all. Instead, Andy helped his mother in her vegetable gardens and sang in school choirs. When, after college, Andy decided to join the Peace Corps, Walter was surprised to hear the organization still existed. He thought it had died with John Kennedy.

There was, however, a time when he did feel connected with Andy. It was the summer between Andy's junior and senior years in college, a few months after Allison, Walter's wife, left him. Andy had begun dating Rebecca Shaw, who lived in a house catty-corner from their backyard in Rocky River. Walter had been friendly with Rebecca's parents ever since they moved to Cleveland from Connecticut.

Rebecca, who is about to enter her final year of law school at Michigan, is slim, blond, attractive, although these aren't the first adjectives Walter would use to describe her. Well-grounded would lead his list. Poised, sensible, *American*—those would follow.

He turns to Gloria, who is staring with wide eyes at the crowd at the bar counter. "What will you do in Spain?" he asks her, and when she doesn't acknowledge him, Andy taps her shoulder and translates the question.

After Gloria and Andy exchange words, Andy says, "We're going to eat and drink our way across Andalucía. And when we're good and full, we'll float across the Mediterranean Sea to Morocco."

"Did *she* say that?" Walter asks. "Or are you putting words in her mouth?"

"It's my rough translation," Andy says. "Really, we haven't planned much." He looks at his watch. "We'd better go."

"I'll walk you to your gate."

"Great."

When they stand, Andy throws an arm around his father's shoulders. "It's good to see you."

"You too," says Walter. And, for the moment, it is good to see Andy. What annoys Walter about Andy is what he also admires about him: his unearned ebullience, his easy faith in the world's pleasures.

When they reach the gate, Gloria needs to use the bathroom, and Andy directs her toward it. When he returns, Walter says, "Listen, Andy, I don't understand how all this happened."

"How what happened?"

"This . . . marriage. When you called to tell me you'd gotten married to some Guatemalan woman, I . . . I couldn't believe it. She's pregnant, I guess."

"Who?"

"Gloria."

Andy laughs, softly at first, then louder, as if enjoying a joke Walter doesn't know he's told. "No, Dad. No." He lets out another brief laugh. "Good try."

"Well, if she isn't . . . Andy, please, explain this to me. You and Rebecca were engaged, and all of the sudden you're married, but to someone else."

There is a pause before Andy says, "You know Rebecca came to visit me in Guatemala."

"I heard she loved it."

"She didn't start off loving it. I had her visit all planned—she insisted on a plan. We were going to spend a few days in the capital before heading up to a bungalow in a cloud forest in Alta Verapaz. On her first night in the country, she complained about the room: It was too cold and it smelled like chlorine. And she was upset because the shower didn't work." Andy shakes his head. "I had to change the itinerary so we would stay in only first-class hotels. And as for the cloud forest and bungalow, well, *adios*."

"I see," Walter says. "You were disappointed because she didn't want to travel like a hobo."

"I wasn't asking her to travel like a hobo. But if she can't bear to go without a shower for even a single day . . . " Andy slows down, smiles: "It was about more than the shower. It was about opening up to new experiences. Anyway, I wasn't going to force her to be miserable. So I broke my piggy bank and we had fun—those air conditioned tour busses can be very relaxing. But I knew she wasn't someone I could spend my life with. I'm not sure I ever thought she was."

"Oh no?" Walter's voice rises. "She's a sensible, smart, attractive woman. And she was willing to marry you. You're a goddamn fool, Andy. A fool, do you understand?"

Andy gives Walter a flat, sympathetic smile. If as a boy he was afraid of Walter's temper, hurrying to the refuge of his mother's or sister's arms, he has learned to overcome it with a meditative calm. Five seconds pass before Andy says, "Dad, I know what you would have done in my place. You would have gone to medical school and married Rebecca. You would be living in a house very much like the one you live in now, and the two of you would have a very comfortable life, I'm sure, until one of you decided you wanted something different, a shock of excitement, and bolted."

Walter readies a rebuttal, but before he can respond, Gloria returns. Motioning behind her, she whispers something to Andy. A moment later, to Walter's surprise, Andy has wrapped his arms around her back and the two of them are gyrating on the thin, gray carpet in the gate area. Gloria giggles, out of nervousness or pleasure, Walter isn't sure.

"There was salsa music playing in the bathroom," Andy explains. "It gave me an idea."

Watching them dance past their carryon bags and toward the broad window at the end of the gate, Walter wishes he could be happy for them. If they were a couple he didn't know, he might think them silly and self-involved, but he would feel none of the concern he feels now. He is certain Andy has made a mistake, and Andy's unwillingness to acknowledge even a small reservation about the reckless course he has chosen leaves Walter feeling mocked.

Walter waits until Andy and Gloria's row is called. Saying good-bye, Andy gives him an extra long hug, as if in forgiveness for their exchange. And turning back to him after he has given his ticket to the woman at the gate, Andy has the last word. "Dad," he says, grinning his generous grin, "why don't *you* marry Rebecca?"

From the oak deck at the back of his house in Rocky River, Walter can see Rebecca Shaw's bedroom window. At night during the winter and spring, the light remained off. But a week and a half before his trip to the Newark Airport and thereafter, it has been on every night beginning around nine. Rebecca is home for the summer because she has an internship at a law firm in downtown Cleveland. Walter doesn't remember the name of the firm, but he knows it doesn't specialize in medical malpractice suits. Rebecca assured him of this when he saw her jogging around the block one morning.

Walter wipes his brow with a handkerchief. He guesses it must be over ninety degrees, and he is thinking of returning to the air conditioning when he hears a low scraping sound. He looks up to see Rebecca standing in the open window, the lilac curtains pulled aside. She fumbles with something in front of her, lifting it to the windowsill. Walter can see it now: a fan. He watches as she attempts to fit it into place, and even from where he's sitting, he can see her over-calculate, pushing the fan to the edge of the screenless window. A nudge, he thinks, and it will fall.

And as if he willed it, it does fall. She clings to air as it drops to the ground, crashing onto the patio below.

"Shit!"

Walter rises from his chair and calls to her: "I'll help you, Rebecca."

She leans out of the window, her hair obscuring her face, and says in a loud whisper, "Who are you?"

"It's Walter."

She pulls her hair behind her head. "Oh, God, Walter, I'm sorry. Did I bother you?"

"I was only sitting here. Let me help."

When she doesn't say anything, he marches across his backyard, cuts across the Levins' yard and steps onto the edge of the Shaws' grass. Although he has been to the Shaws' house a dozen times, he has never come this way, like a child or thief would.

He picks up the window fan from the brick patio. Its white plastic face has split off, leaving the fan blades exposed. Rebecca pulls open a sliding door and steps onto the patio. She is wearing blue jeans and a T-shirt and no shoes.

"I think it's dead," Walter says. "Or at least critically injured." He holds up the separated face. "You might be able to Superglue this back on, but I'm not sure how safe it would be."

She takes a few steps toward him to examine the damage. "It was an old fan anyway," she says. "I wouldn't need it, except our air conditioning broke. My dad warned me the system was acting up, but of course he and my mom are off on vacation when it finally quits."

"You can have someone fix it tomorrow."

"I will." She takes another step toward him. He notices how small her feet are. "I'm sorry to have bothered you," she says.

"You didn't bother me."

A silence follows, and Walter listens to the shrill hum of crickets.

"I understand Andy got married," Rebecca says.

"Yes, he did."

"I hope he's happy."

"He's always happy." Walter speaks with disdain, as if he'd said his son is always high or drunk. He is aware of how absurd his implied criticism must seem. "I have to say I was disappointed in who he married."

"Why?"

"Because," Walter says simply, "he wasn't marrying you."

"Oh." She looks away, and Walter wonders if he has embarrassed her. When she turns back to him, he sees a small smile on her face.

"It's true," he says, grateful to be speaking with someone who can, at last, appreciate his point of view. "I even told him so when I saw him and his wife in Newark the other day."

She says softly, "Maybe that wasn't the most tactful thing to say."

"I didn't say it in front of his wife," he amends. "But you're right. It wasn't going to change the situation. I guess I just needed to say it—for the record, as it were."

"Well, I appreciate your vote of confidence."

He asks about her work, and she tells him about the long hours and the best perk—the daily luncheon spread catered by Giovanni's. He tells her about one of his patients, a man who acquired a startling rash while, on a bet, trying to swim two miles in Lake Erie. He asks where her parents have gone, and she says, "Alaska—where it's probably nice and cool right now."

After they say goodnight and turn toward their houses, Walter wheels around and says, "If you find you're too hot, you're welcome to stay at my house. As you know, I have a guest room, and the air conditioner is working."

"Thank you, Walter. I should be all right." She hauls her broken fan into the house.

From his back porch, he sees her bedroom light click on again, glowing against the lilac curtains. Between waves of cricket songs, he thinks he can hear her undress, the easy sound of peeling clothes.

At eight-thirty the next evening, Rebecca is standing outside his door. "I couldn't sleep last night," she says, and he sees how weary she looks—her purplish eyelids, the limpness of her blond hair. "The air conditioning people said they wouldn't be able to come until next week, and I got home from work too late to buy a window fan."

"Come in," he says.

"I'm sorry to bother you. I don't know if you were serious about your offer last night."

"Of course I was serious. And you're not bothering me."

When she is inside and sitting on his chocolate-colored leather couch, she says, sighing, "I could barely keep my eyes open today, even after three cups of coffee. And I heard the temperature is supposed to stay at ninety-something all night."

He excuses himself to make up the guest room, but before he's halfway up the stairs, he remembers it's already made up. He thought he might convince Andy and his wife to come to Cleveland after all.

Downstairs with Rebecca again, he says, "I'd offer you a drink, but I expect you'd rather go straight to bed."

"Please," she says with relief. "If you don't mind."

He shows her to the guest room, an unnecessary courtesy. She is familiar with the house, which has remained unchanged since Allison left, since Rebecca and Andy dated.

He says goodnight to her, and she again thanks him. He returns downstairs and hears her use the bathroom, hears her shut the guest room door, hears her click off the bedside reading light.

When, half an hour later, he climbs the stairs to his room, he stops outside her door. He listens for her breathing. What he hears is his own, an accompaniment to the beating of his heart.

The next evening, she comes bearing a bottle of wine. "I wanted to thank you for last night," she says.

"You did," he says, "several times. Come in."

"I shouldn't."

"You don't expect me to drink this all by myself, do you?"

"Well . . ."

"Humor me," he says.

She sits on the couch and he sits across from her in an armchair. He feels an easiness between them. They share something: their befuddlement over Andy. In the morning, over breakfast, they'd shared stories about Andy, laughed about his relentless optimism.

After pouring the wine, he says, "Did you find a window fan?"

Rebecca blushes. "Well, I . . . " She pauses. "I left work too late to shop for one. But I'll be fine tonight. It's supposed to be a little cooler, and, thanks to you, I had a good sleep last night."

"Please, Rebecca. I have this entire house cooled to seventy-two degrees. I'd be insulted if you didn't stay here again."

She gives him a look, and he is conscious of something different in it. If he's right, it's an appraising look, a look to see if they might be on different ground than they were the previous night.

Instead of playing golf in the afternoon, as he'd planned, he drove to his health club and lifted weights and rode a stationary bike until his thighs throbbed. After his shower, he stood naked in front of the long mirror in the locker room, and he was pleased to see how fit he looked. If the hair on his head is turning gray, his chest hair remains decidedly dark, and his waist looks like it belongs to a thirty-five-year-old instead of to someone three years shy of fifty.

"All right," she says, smiling. "I'm a wimp—I'll admit it. I can't live without air conditioning."

"You shouldn't have to," Walter says. "This is America after all."

She blushes again. "Andy must have told you about my trip to Guatemala."

"He mentioned it."

"I guess I spoiled it for him, acting like a princess."

"I expect he wanted you to act like a peasant. You had a right to be comfortable." Walter lifts his glass of wine. "To America," he says, and they drink. She finishes her glass in three sips, and he refills it.

"I guess I disappointed him," she says. "I wasn't tough enough."

Walter scoffs. "I think he thought of himself as Tarzan and was expecting you to be Jane. Wait until his wife tastes the good life in Spain. She won't want to swing from the vines in Guatemala anymore."

"It's obvious Andy thought I was too conventional."

Walter chuckles. "I think Andy is confusing conventionality with good sense."

They have, before long, finished the wine. "Let me open another bottle," he says, and when she doesn't object, he retrieves one from a rack in the kitchen. When he returns, he drops next to her on the couch to refill her glass.

Rebecca asks about Andy's wife, and Walter tells her what he knows about Gloria and how easily distracted she seemed in the Newark Airport, like a child drawn to whatever bright light flashed next. "She'll keep Andy scrambling to entertain her," Walter says, although he knows he's being uncharitable, mean even. And he doesn't share with Rebecca the last scene of Gloria and Andy dancing on the dull carpet in the gate area, their bodies silhouetted against the broad, smoke-stained window. In idle moments in the last few days, it is the image he has found himself lingering over.

He asks Rebecca if she is dating anyone, and she shakes her head and says she is too busy at school and now work to have much of a social life.

They talk about what she'll do after she finishes law school— she hopes to be hired by the firm she's interning for, maybe meet someone down the line.

He asks about her parents, and the topic leads them to talking about when they first saw each other. Rebecca says, "I didn't believe you were Andy's real father."

"Why?"

"You looked too different from him—and too young."

"It's nice of you to lie."

"I'm serious."

Walter knows it is the wine talking. All the same, he is happy to play along. "You're just saying that because I have air conditioning."

She laughs. "Oh, no. Andy always used to say he was cheated when he didn't inherit your looks."

"I trained him to say that so that he *would* inherit my money."

"I'm being honest." She laughs in the silly way wine makes people laugh and puts her hand on his knee, a friendly, emphatic pat.

"My ego thanks you."

She says, "It's all in the name of air conditioning, remember?" Her hand finds his knee again and stays there. "Well," she says, "I better go grab some sleep while your offer's still good."

"Sleep well," he says.

He lifts her hand and kisses it. He recognizes the gesture as an invitation, prompted by his own wine drinking—the wine, anyway, is the excuse he would use if challenged. "Goodnight, Rebecca." She hesitates, and he feels a strange undulation in his chest, a seesaw of panic and hope. She leans toward him and kisses him on the lips. Her kiss stuns him with its warmth and softness, and he feels himself go still, whatever was unbalanced within him righted.

"Goodnight, Walter," she says, but she doesn't leave his couch.

He remains inert, as if his mind needs time to apprehend his good fortune before sending impulses to his limbs to act on it. At last, he leans into her, a quick movement—his body shocked to life, released—and kisses her. She allows his lips to linger, encouraging them with her own.

She pulls back, giggling. "I don't know what I'm doing. Will you tell me?"

"Only if you tell me what I'm doing," he says.

After a few minutes, his hands slide under her blouse to unsnap, with an old ease, her bra.

In his bed, he is worried about his performance—it has been six months, a one-night stand with a divorced colleague at a conference in Minneapolis, and he isn't sober—but when she touches him, he responds, and he remains hard even after he breaks to pull a condom from his dresser drawer.

When she says, "I've come, Walter, it's your turn," he can't. He doesn't want this to end. But supposing there is a proper arc to pleasure, a point at which it turns to routine and work, he fakes orgasm for the first time in his life.

All day, between patients, he wonders what she is thinking. He wonders if she'll accuse him of taking advantage of her, plying her with alcohol in order to seduce her. He wonders if her reaction will be more mild but equally dismissive, if she'll regret sleeping with a man her parents' age—one of her parents' friends, for God's sake. In other moments, he thinks she'll come to his house again tonight, and they'll joke about heat and air conditioning before finding their way upstairs.

He wonders if he should send her flowers at work, but he doesn't remember the name of her law firm, and he thinks flowers might embarrass her. Instead, when he comes home at six, he leaves a single red rose on her doorstep with an unsigned note: "The air is cool, the door is open."

He sits on his couch, flipping through a copy of the *Norton Anthology of American Poetry*, which he discovered in Andy's old bedroom. He reads a few of the poems without understanding them. He fixes himself a light dinner: spaghetti and Italian bread and a salad of red peppers, tomatoes and spinach. He brushes his teeth and dabs on cologne.

It's eight-thirty, and she hasn't come. He steps onto his back porch and is disappointed to find the night air, though heavy, tolerable. With an open window, a person might sleep with no problem at all. He feels betrayed by nature.

He returns to his couch and his book of poetry. His eyes make contact with the words, but again they make no sense. Thinking his watch might have decided to speed up on its own accord, he goes to the kitchen to verify the time on the microwave. Nine-twenty-six.

He has nodded off when he hears a faint tapping at the front door. She is outside, prim in her navy blue suit, but her hair is down, frizzy, as if electrified by the humidity. "You lied in your note."

"I did?"

"Your door wasn't open."

Walter smiles. "It is now."

He lives two lives, one when he is without Rebecca—working or at the gym, where he always stops in front of the bathroom mirror, examining the hair on his body the way he did when it first grew, a curious, magnificent sprouting—and one when he is with her, when all his senses are alive, as if someone had thrown on a switch in his heart.

On Saturday night, he takes her to Mirabella's, a Mexican restaurant on Lake Erie. The walls are decorated with impressionistic paintings of bullfights, and the tables sprout white, yellow, and red carnations. The decor, after they've dipped into the chips and salsa, inspires talk of interior decorating. For her future home, Rebecca knows exactly what she wants—in the living room, hardwood floors, walls painted a light gold, Oriental rugs, a coffee-colored leather couch with matching armchair. "And I want some kind of antique coffee table," she says, "something in cherrywood, very solid." She describes the other rooms—the stainless steel kitchen, the bathroom with a bidet, which, she says, "I've wanted ever since I went to Paris on an eighth-grade trip."

"Go on," he says, and he follows her past the library, with its complete set of the Harvard Classics, and into the bedroom, where the king-sized bed and its honey-colored sheets rests beneath a skylight.

Later, in his bed with its white sheets and decade-old quilt, one his wife bought in Maine, they make love, lie in each other's arms, separate. The lights are off, and it's a dark night. He can't see her beside him—he barely hears her breathing.

She says, "Did you ever think of an answer?"

"To what?"

"To what I'm doing?"

"Oh," he says. "Yes, I have."

"Tell me."

His first impulse is to say "Living," but this seems either too grandiose or too banal. He opts for a joke: "You're staying cool."

The air conditioning jokes have become old, he knows. She laughs nonetheless, grateful, it seems, to keep their conversation this easy.

On Sunday afternoon, he grills salmon seasoned with soy sauce, and they eat on the back porch. After they've finished dinner and a bottle of Merlot, he asks, "What are we going to do when your parents come home?"

An uncomfortable look flashes across her face before she gives him an assured smile. "They won't be home for three days."

He would like to press the subject with her, but he suspects she is puzzling it over herself, weighing her feelings, contemplating outcomes. He doesn't want to intrude prematurely on her deliberations.

When she says, "I'm going to make it an early night—it's back to work tomorrow," he follows her to bed but, when she's sleeping, returns downstairs and pours himself a quarter glass of brandy. He plots how he'll tell her parents, working on the words he'll use. He needs an introduction to his speech, but he knows its heart: *I am as serious about your daughter as I've ever been about anyone in my life.*

At three in the afternoon the next day, she calls him at his office: "I wanted to let you know I'm going out for drinks with some people at work."

"Okay," he says. "I'll leave the door open."

"You don't have to. I can sleep at my place tonight."

"I wouldn't think of it. Besides, it's supposed to stay hot all night."

"Don't wait up," she says. "I'd feel bad."

"Okay," he says. "I won't."

He does wait up, although he debates whether this is the right strategy. He should pretend indifference, he thinks. But it has been a long time since he has had to mark his moves in a relationship, to strike the right balance between interest and nonchalance. He pours a glass of brandy and opens the *Norton Anthology*. He looks for poems he knows and stops on T.S. Eliot's "The Love Song of J. Alfred Prufrock." *In the rooms the women come and go, talking of Michelangelo.*

The line leads him to thinking about the last time he visited the Cleveland Museum of Art. It was probably when Andy was in junior high school.

Now he wants to do what he hasn't done in years—walk the marble floors of the art museum, sink into the plush seats of Severance Hall and listen to a Mozart symphony. He wants to buy bleacher tickets and lounge in the sunshine in Jacobs Field, he wants to sail a Sunfish on Lake Erie. He pictures himself doing all this with Rebecca, and as the brandy sinks into him, warming him, he pretends she is sitting next to him, listening to the options, consenting to each with a quick, enthusiastic nod.

It's eleven o'clock, a quarter after, eleven thirty, and his brandy-borne elation fades, replaced by tiredness and the beginnings of worry. Where is she?

Thinking she might have gone to her house, he stands, steps up to the glass door leading to the back porch and stares across the night. Her house is dark, a comfort. He returns to the couch, pours a few drops of brandy into his glass and drinks.

Her voice wakes him up. "You should have gone to bed."

He needs a moment to shake away his dreams, reorient himself. She is sitting next to him.

"I was reading," he says.

"It couldn't have been very exciting."

"It was, actually," he says, "but I guess I've become used to more exciting evenings."

She laughs, a slow, long laugh, and he guesses she is still under the influence of whatever she drank tonight.

"What time is it?" he asks.

"Late." She touches his shoulder. "I was thinking about going home, but when my friends asked me where I wanted to be dropped off, I gave them directions here."

"I'm glad."

"I had a little too much to drink," she says. "I don't usually do that." She sounds apologetic, almost ashamed, and he thinks she might be asking for his pardon.

"I know you don't," he says.

"God, I'm tired. Could you be sure to wake me up at seven, Walter? I'm worried about sleeping through the alarm."

"I'll wake you up. Don't worry."

"Thank you." She touches his shoulder again, squeezing it twice before leaning her head against it. Nestled awkwardly, she closes her eyes.

"We should go upstairs," he says.

"Carry me," she says, her eyes still closed.

He doesn't know if she is serious, but awake now and eager to meet whatever challenges she presents him, he kneels in front of her, puts his right arm under her legs, his left arm around her back, and lifts. Her weight surprises him, and he releases an involuntary grunt, but he steadies himself, keeping his knees bent.

"I was joking, Walter." She gazes up at him, her eyelids battling the light. "Please don't have a heart attack."

He tries to laugh, but what comes out is another grunt. Unsteadily, but with determination, he moves toward the staircase. He smells the cigarette smoke in her hair. As he ascends the stairs, she laughs, with pleasure or with gentle mockery or in fear of being dropped, he isn't sure, but he perseveres to the top, laying her on his bed.

"My champion," she declares.

When he returns from the bathroom after brushing his teeth, she is asleep. He removes her shoes and brings a light cotton blanket from his closet and settles it over her.

"Goodnight," he whispers, although he himself doesn't fall asleep for hours.

The next evening, Rebecca comes to his house soon after he arrives home from work. She is wearing a maroon suit, and her hair is pulled behind her head. He sees a faint covering of powder on her face.

She is carrying a plastic bag. "I brought Indian food for us," she says.

"Great," he says, stepping aside to let her in. "You know," he says, "I should give you a key to the house."

She says, "I wanted to apologize for last night. I shouldn't have come over."

"I'm glad you did."

"I kept you up."

"You didn't keep me up—you woke me up."

She goes to the kitchen, and when he follows her, she says, "Sit down. I'll fix dinner." She gives a light laugh. "I guess 'fix' isn't the right word. Pour, maybe? Un-carton?"

Over dinner, he asks her what kind of art she likes, whether she likes baseball or sailing. She answers politely, briefly.

After a silence, she says, "Have you heard from Andy?"

"A postcard from Spain. He and Gloria went water skiing on some river—and Gloria doesn't even know how to swim."

He is hopeful about engaging her in this topic, their familiar, gentle critique of Andy and his heedlessness, but she again falls silent.

"I'll sleep at my place tonight," she says after a while. "I'm so tired, I don't think I'd be much company."

"Don't worry about it," he says. "I'm going to call it an early night myself. We'll watch a *Seinfeld* re-run and go to bed. What do you think?"

She eats the last of her chicken curry and looks up at him. Responding to his smile, she smiles a little herself. "Okay, Walter," she says. "Sure."

And this is exactly what they do. In its very ordinariness the night seems, to Walter, extraordinary. It's barely ten o'clock, and here she is, beside him again, asleep.

The night before Rebecca's parents are due home, he grills swordfish with red peppers and mushrooms. Afterward, filled with good food and good wine, they make love on the back porch. He didn't foresee this—he has never been adventurous when it comes to sex—but they'd ended up kissing after finishing the last of the wine, and after a scramble to undo each other's jeans, she'd climbed on top of him as he sat on a bench against the porch's rail. "Don't worry," she says when he asks her about birth control, "my period's due tomorrow." Somewhere between penetration and orgasm, he wonders if Andy and Gloria have ever done something this exposed, this bold. This trumps, easily, their airport dance, more than matches their water-skiing.

When they've finished, Rebecca doesn't remain long on top of him. "It's actually cold out here," she says.

She retreats to the bathroom off the kitchen. He hears the water running, and he knows what she's doing: washing herself, soaking up the scent they made together into a hand cloth. When she emerges from the bathroom, she looks as dainty and distant as a bank teller. He usually admires this about her, her properness, but now he wants her to be sloppy about their improprieties and lust, to let them hang on her like white foam on a wave.

She settles into his couch, close to him, but not in his arms.

"That," he says, nodding toward the backyard porch, "was wonderful."

"The swordfish?" she asks, and winks.

He wants her closer, and he puts his arm around her, pulling her to him. He feels her resist before she concedes, relaxes.

"We'll have to go public when your parents come home," he says.

"Ah," she murmurs.

"But they'll understand, I'm sure of it." He is about to tell her about the speech he has prepared for her parents, but when he turns to look at her, she seems distracted, as if she were listening to a television playing somewhere else in the house. He knows something is off, something he should ponder. "I know it's early in our . . . our relationship, but I have to tell you, Rebecca, I feel very happy when I'm with you. I know there might be a few awkward spots to overcome, what with your past relationship with Andy and your parents, but if I'm reading this right . . . ."

He can feel her stiffen, and he knows before she can tell him, knows he has leaped when he should have inched ahead.

She says, "I think we'll have to slow down, Walter."

"You're right," he says, retreating quickly, "I didn't mean to come on too fast, like a high school boy."

"I mean," she says, "we need to stop."

The last word flattens him. He feels his body tingle and grow numb.

"This is about the craziest thing I've ever done," she says, "but I can't keep doing it. I have another year of law school left, and . . . ."

He says, "I understand. You might meet someone. But if you don't . . . "

"Walter," she says, and he wonders how often Andy heard her speak like this, like a schoolteacher chiding a student. "Walter, this won't work—long-term, I mean."

"Why?" His question is less plaintive than curious. He wants to know where he failed.

"You're older than I am. You're my parents' age. I do find you attractive, obviously, and I don't regret what we did. Like I said, it's the craziest thing I've ever done, and tonight topped the list." She gestures toward the backyard porch and smiles ruefully, as if recalling something in the distant past. "But my parents will have the air conditioning fixed, if I even need air conditioning now anymore, and I'll go back to doing what I was doing."

"Which was what?"

She looks at him with surprise, then answers patiently: "To building my future."

He is stumped. The house of her dreams . . . was he wrong to consider himself at least a candidate for the armchair in the living room, for the space beside her beneath the honey-colored sheets? "I thought . . . ." He stops, worried about where his unplanned words will take him. But what does it matter now? He has been let go, so he can let go. "I thought I might be considered a potential part of that future."

She turns to him with a look of what he decides is manu-factured sympathy. Or perhaps it's real sympathy, the facile sympathy of someone who is used to having absolute control over her emotions and has never allowed herself to approach, much less be swallowed by, real joy or despair.

"I never thought you'd consider it possible, us being together any longer than a few weeks," she says. "I mean, I thought you understood where I was in my life." She shakes her head slowly. "I'm sorry, Walter."

"I don't understand," he says, "why you even started this . . . this . . . ." He searches for the proper word to describe what they've shared, what they've done. He settles, unsatisfactorily, on *fling*.

She doesn't reply immediately, and he mulls over her reasons. Perhaps she wanted revenge against Andy. Yes, of course she did, and he is about to accuse her of this when she says, "You're an attractive man, Walter. I guess I've always had a little crush on you. And you always seemed to like me—even more than Andy liked me. So, against my better judgment, I did this. I had this . . . this fling. Okay?"

He puts his hand under her chin and lifts it. He stares into her cool blue eyes and speaks like a man already gone, spinning down the vortex of her past. Perhaps she has heard the words he is about to speak, perhaps she has heard them from his own flesh and blood. Andy might have spoken them to her on their first night together in Guatemala as they shivered in the sheets, a plea to push her toward danger, adventure, the shores of life where risk meets pleasure. Even if he's using borrowed words, plagiarizing from his son, he knows it will be the best speech of his life because it will be the last of its kind he'll ever give, every word a passionate grab for life, dangerous and savage and soul-saving life.

"Rebecca," he begins, and in speaking just her name, he realizes how unrecognizably deep and resonant his voice has become, how rough and powerful in its unleashing. And his words carry him, as if on a current, toward what he most wants, toward the rest of his life.

"I'm going to swim it," Sam told his wife as they stared across the river to the slab of rock on the other side. Lit up in the sunlight, the rock looked inviting.

At first, his wife said nothing. When, at last, she spoke, he realized she didn't think he was serious: "Butterfly or breaststroke?"

"I can do it."

"Come on, Sam, the current's too fast. Besides, it's probably a hundred yards to the rock." She patted his waist, which had expanded by an inch or two in the past few years. "When was the last time you went swimming?" she asked, but already he was removing his T-shirt and jeans and slipping on his suit.

"Please, Sam," she said in a voice he'd heard more than a few times in his life, the times he'd proposed doing something she considered even mildly outrageous. He pulled the cords of his orange swimsuit tight. He'd never worn the suit, and it had the bright look of unused clothing.

"Please don't, Sam."

"Come on, Laura. I used to do this all the time in the Peace Corps."

"That was ten years ago." She grabbed him by the elbow. "Besides, no one's around here to help me rescue you."

They had left their guide, Eugenio, a few hundred yards up the river. He was preparing lunch.

Sam shook off his wife's hand. "Let me have a little adventure, all right?"

She released her hand and took a step back. He expected her to remind him that he was a father, that his two daughters relied on him to make sane decisions. She said nothing, however.

Good, he thought. I'll spend half an hour on the rock while she sulks in the shade.

He dropped his feet into the water, which was colder than he'd expected. Too cold maybe. But he couldn't turn back now. He glanced behind him. Laura wasn't even looking at him, but was clearing a place to sit beneath a pine tree.

He pushed off the bank and into the bone-cold water. He felt his heart respond to the icy assault. Although he was tempted to cry out in surprise, he didn't want to give his wife cause to gloat. He moved his arms and legs, stroking toward the rock.

After ten seconds, he knew he was in trouble. The current was faster than it had seemed and he was spending more energy fighting it than he was using to advance across the river. *Turn back*, a voice inside him said. He didn't listen. He didn't want to see his wife triumph because of his cowardice.

He felt his energy flagging. It was an odd sensation—his brain was telling his body to continue, but his body had given up hope and was only hacking at the water. He thought to call for help. Too late: his limbs went numb and darkness pounded against his eyes. My God, he thought, I'm finished.

He found himself lying on his back, his head at rest against sand. He'd washed up against a bank, although the bottom half of his body was still in the water. Above him, twenty-five yards up stream, was a waterfall. He must have gone over it, although he didn't know how he'd survived. The waterfall was at least five stories.

He knew this exact spot. As a Peace Corps volunteer, he'd traveled here on several occasions, usually with Consuela, his Guatemalan girlfriend. She'd been pretty, with short, black hair, a small nose and wide, brown eyes. She'd never let him make love to her. She had to save herself, she said, for her husband.

He wondered if he'd made a mistake in not marrying her. He doubted she would have liked the States, but they might have stayed in Guatemala. He could have taken over her father's shoe factory.

Despite his awkward position on the sandy bank, he felt no urge to leave. He knew he should try to move his legs, however, to test whether he was paralyzed. When he was able to stand, he didn't celebrate. He was numb to the miracle of his survival.

He staggered up the bank and into the shelter of trees. A moment later, he heard his name called. He knew the voice, Laura's, but he didn't feel the need to respond to it. He heard

Eugenio's voice as well. Without knowing what he was doing, he moved higher into the woods, hiding behind a pair of *ceiba* trees.

In a minute, he heard his wife and Eugenio pass below him. They were walking on the riverbank. His wife spoke little Spanish and Eugenio no English, but their rescue efforts didn't require much communication. They were both yelling, "Sam! Sam!"

He waited until he heard their voices a good distance downstream before turning back upstream. He stayed in the forest, parallel to the river. It took him fifteen minutes, he guessed, before he reached the spot where he and Laura had been sitting. In her panic, she had left everything: clothes, cameras, money. He gathered everything into a backpack.

A short distance upstream, he found the Range Rover they had rented and the blanket where Eugenio had set their lunches. Sam devoured a ham sandwich before packing the rest of the food into another, smaller backpack.

With the two backpacks, one slung over each shoulder, he made his way down from the mountain. Instead of keeping to the main road, he stayed on a trail he'd known as a Peace Corps volunteer and had walked several times with Consuela, kissing her in the shade of fiddlehead ferns. He'd wanted more from her than her lips, and the thought of what he'd missed inspired him now. He wanted a day with her, he wanted a day with his old life.

An hour later, he was sitting in the shade of a fiddlehead fern, thinking of Consuela, when he heard the Range Rover drive past on the road below. It was the only machine sound in a forest filled with birdsongs and the buzzing of mosquitoes. He guessed his wife and Eugenio were going to the town at the bottom of the mountain to call a rescue team. It pleased him to think of his wife's distress, although at the same time he knew she must be thinking, with a certain measure of righteousness, *I told him not to swim it.*

By the time he reached town thirty minutes later, there was no sign of the Range Rover. He had expected it to be parked in the town square. In fact, he half expected his wife to spot him, looking ragged from his watery brush with death and his climb down the mountain, and run to embrace him. He would claim amnesia before wrapping his arms around her in a scene of emotional reunion.

He stood in the middle of the square. A dozen people were sitting on benches and two boys were playing marbles in the shade of a kiosk, but no one looked up at him. No one pointed at him and shouted, "There's the dead man!"

He thought of going to inquire about his wife and Eugenio in one of the *tiendas* off the square before he remembered his resolve to return to the town where he'd lived. His wife, wherever she was, would have to live a day thinking he was dead.

A bus was idling at the end of the town square, and he walked toward it, looking back several times before stepping on.

It was a little after three o'clock when he arrived in San Cristóbal. From inside the broken-down tollbooth at the town entrance, Don Francisco greeted him as if he'd seen him yesterday. "Don Samuel!" the old man saluted. "Come join me for a drink."

As always, Sam refused. "You'll drink yourself to death," Sam said, his usual line, and Don Francisco replied, as he always had, "It hasn't killed me yet."

Sam walked up the dirt road toward the center of town with the old man cackling behind him. Before long, he was met by a pair of children, a boy and girl. "Don Samuel!" they shouted gleefully. They couldn't have been older than eight and wouldn't have been alive when he'd lived in San Cristóbal. Nevertheless, he greeted them as if he knew them, and they smiled.

At Pensión El Lago, Doña Amalia, the owner, hadn't aged at all. She had the same narrow face with smooth skin and long, dark hair. She looked up at him from behind the counter. "Don Samuel," she said. "How are you?"

He told her he was well and was glad to be back in town.

"When did you leave?" she asked.

"Ten years ago."

"Nooo," she said, funneling her lips into a small *o*. "I don't believe it."

Apparently, she really didn't believe it, because when he asked for a room, she said, "But what about your house?"

"I left it ten years ago."

"You sold it?"

"I never owned it. I rented it from Don Augusto."

Doña Amalia seemed to consider this. "I'm sure he would rent it to you again."

He thought the house was probably occupied, although the idea of renting his old house had a definite appeal. "I'll talk with him tomorrow," he said. "But I need a place to stay today."

Doña Amalia handed him a key to one of the rooms, chiding him: "You aren't going to use it to meet the beautiful Consuela?"

He was about to explain that he had a wife—he had the ring on his finger to prove it—but decided it wasn't worth the effort. He shook his head and walked to his room at the back of the *pensión*.

After showering, he put on a clean pair of khakis and a dark blue T-shirt. He had combed his brown hair, which had thinned some in ten years. He wished he had cologne to dabble on his neck. Consuela always liked his cologne.

When he walked back past the desk in the front of the *pensión*, Doña Amalia said, "I know where you're going," and winked.

Outside, the town smelled as he remembered: of bus exhaust, bougainvillea and the faint, sweet-sickening smell of shoe dye. He looked to his right and saw Don Geronimo's shoe factory, propped in the hills above the lake. From a distance, it looked like a castle. In another life, it would have been his castle.

He thought of Laura and wondered where she'd gone in the Range Rover. Perhaps she'd already given up on him, considered him dead. Perhaps she was at the airport, waiting to fly back to the States. What would she tell their daughters?

He tried to picture the two of them, Bernice and Allison. Bernice was five and Allison was two. They were beautiful children, but he couldn't remember exactly what they looked like. Bernice had his brown hair, he believed, although, on second thought, she might have favored Laura, whose hair was reddish-blond. Allison was too small to look much like anyone yet. When he tried to picture her, only the face of a generic two-year-old, bright-cheeked and small-eyed, came to mind.

When I go back home, he thought, I'll have to do better. I'll have to look at them, really look at them.

He would leave San Cristóbal tomorrow and return to the States. He had to see his daughters. Besides, if Laura thought he was dead, he wondered how much time she would spend in mourning him before she started up with Charlie, their former classmate at Oberlin. He lived not far from them on the west side of Cleveland.

Walking around San Cristóbal, he remembered this kind of late afternoon light, pieces of sunlight dropping through the rain clouds. It would rain soon, and people were hurrying their business, rushing home from the market with vegetables and cans of *frijoles negros*. He walked quickly toward Consuela's house, located on the opposite side of the lake from her father's shoe factory.

He reached Consuela's door just as the rains began, both soothing and swift, chasing off whoever remained on the street. He watched the rain drive the dust from the cobblestones, leaving them slick and clean. He remembered all this from years before, but in the interim, he'd forgotten it. He thought, Look at how much I've lost without even knowing it.

Although Consuela lived in her parents' two-story house, she had a private room and entrance on the first floor. As he lifted his hand to knock, he wondered how many men had made the same pilgrimage in the last ten years, and how many of them had been rewarded.

She opened the door instantly. If she wasn't exactly the same, she was close. Perhaps she was a little heavier. Perhaps her face was narrower from age. She'd be only thirty years old now, he thought, hardly an old maid, even in Guatemala. No, she was the same, and he had the same feelings he'd had when he'd first fallen in love with her, the same inarticulateness. He stood at her door like a mute supplicant hoping to be rewarded with a few centavos.

Her face showed an instant of surprise, a streak of delight, before settling again into her familiar look of faint curiosity. "Samuel," she said, stepping aside. "*Pase adelante.*"

To be in her room again was like stepping back in time. Everything was the same as it was when he'd left her, the same as it probably had been since she was thirteen. The vanity mirror adorning the far wall had the same dozen stickers on the wood frame, cartoon bears and cats giving Valentine greetings. On top of the bookshelf in the corner were her basketball trophies. She'd been the star of her high school team, and she had the hardware to prove it. On the wall above her bed, located at the end of the room, was the same framed picture of Jesus, his head bowed as if in contemplation of whoever was sleeping below.

He sat on the small couch in front of a table in the middle of the room, and when she'd finished preparing coffee on the burner in the corner, she joined him. She said, "How are you?"

He hadn't expected the verb tense and was prepared to answer, "I've been all right." Instead, he found himself talking about seeing Don Francisco and Doña Amalia earlier in the day.

"They're exactly the same," he said, expressing his wonder.

She said, "Very little changes."

"But I've changed," Sam said.

"No," she said, looking at him. "You haven't changed." She reached to touch his hair, a quick flick across his forehead, the way she used to. "You are the same."

"In a few years," he said, "I'll be bald." But even as he said this, he noticed in the mirror across the way that his hair wasn't as thin as he'd thought. Perhaps the dark room had something to do with this. All the same, he felt he'd fooled time. Inspired by his deception, he reached for Consuela's hand, holding it between his two palms, the way he used to do. As he did so, he was startled to feel his wedding band. She wore no ring of her own, and he was glad she didn't seem to notice his.

"How are you?" he asked, purposely using the same tense she had.

"I'm well."

"Are you still working at your father's shoe factory?" After she'd graduated from high school, Consuela had become her father's secretary and accountant.

"Yes."

They drank their coffee. As usual, she wouldn't look directly at him. This was a Guatemalan woman's way of being modest, and he liked it, especially after his wife's constant intrusions into his life.

"I was at the waterfalls in Lanquín today," he said.

She glanced at him and gave him a slight pout. "And you didn't invite me?"

"Would you have come?"

"Maybe."

He felt his heart beat with a familiar joy and anticipation. This was their courtship banter, the dance they'd danced until he'd finished his two-year tour in Guatemala and had gone home to marry Laura. But if he couldn't return to the past, might he simply resume where he'd stopped?

He reached for her hand again. "It's good to see you."

Blushing, she turned away. As he bent to kiss her cheek, he heard the door open. He quickly moved away as two boys, one about six years old, the other about four, stepped into the room. Their black hair was damp from the rain.

"*Abuela* says dinner is ready," the older boy said. Although he was obviously addressing Consuela, he was looking at Sam. There was no hostility in his eyes, only curiosity and a kind of hope.

"All right," Consuela said, and the boys disappeared as quickly as they'd come.

Sam turned to her. "Your sons?"

She nodded, although barely. She might only have been keeping time to a faint beat from the music playing from the street.

He wanted to ask when she'd had them and who the father was and where he was now, but Consuela interrupted his thoughts: "Please have dinner with us."

A minute later, Sam found himself sitting where he'd sat on several occasions, in a hard chair in front of a mahogany table in a dining room with a tile floor. As usual, he sat next to Don Geronimo, a tall, heavyset man with a tan, lined face and large, sun-chapped lips. Although a factory owner, Don Geronimo spent little time at his business. He preferred to go horseback riding, galloping off into the mountains to the west.

Only Sam, Don Geronimo, and Consuela sat at the table. Consuela's mother, Doña Inez, served the meal of chicken, rice and beets but didn't sit down. She moved continually from the dining room to the kitchen, refilling Don Geronimo's plate and cup of coffee. Sam had no idea where Consuela's sons had gone.

After asking Sam how he was, Don Geronimo began to pontificate about his favorite topic: his shoe factory and the laziness of his workers. "Coming from the United States, you don't know how difficult it is to handle people like this. In the United States, people are hardworking and trustworthy. Here, they are all *ladrones*." He emphasized the point by rubbing his thumb against his index finger. "They have robbed me of thousands."

He paused to eat a spoonful of beets. "But of course I do not have the temperament nor the youth to oversee the factory as I should." He gave Sam a knowing look. "Now, if one day you and Consuela should decide to . . . ." He glanced at his daughter, who smiled back at him, before turning again to Sam. "Well, I'm sure you would do an excellent job in my place. As you know it's the only shoe factory in all of Alta Verapaz."

Sam had to force himself not to laugh. He already had a job—he managed a hat factory in Cleveland—and, more significant, he already had a wife. To have revealed these facts, however, would have been to ruin the spirit of the meal, which Sam was enjoying precisely because it seemed to presume that nothing had transpired in the last ten years.

Before long, Sam was nodding at what Don Geronimo was saying and even contemplating how he might, in fact, resume the life he'd left. Perhaps his wife believed he was dead. Maybe he would have the opportunity to start again.

After dinner, he and Consuela walked outside. The rain had stopped, leaving the air cool and fresh. He walked her to her door, as he'd done a hundred times before.

In the light from the bulb above her door, he saw her glorious hair, her smooth skin, her thin lips. They had missed ten years of each other's lives—a full one-third of their time on earth—but she had decided to ignore this, and he didn't know why he shouldn't follow her lead. He kissed her, the same brief, fiery kiss they'd always exchanged at her doorstep. He was hot with anticipation. He pulsed with the promise of the future.

Returning to Pensión El Lago, Sam found Doña Amalia behind the counter. He asked about the father of Consuela's children.

"They aren't yours?" she replied, giving him a bright smile.

From her expression, he couldn't tell whether she was joking.

He shook his head and retreated to his room, unsure what to think. He wondered where Laura was and how their daughters were doing. He had trouble picturing anything about his life in the States. And when he'd undressed and slipped under the rough, wool blanket in the single bed, he didn't think of his family but of Consuela and how soft and appealing her lips were and how he wanted more.

In the morning, he walked to the Guatel office near the lake and put a handful of twenty-five-centavo coins in the slot above the pay phone. When he dialed his home number, however, no one answered. Thinking he might have misdialed, he tried again. Same result.

After collecting his coins, he walked up the street to where Don Augusto lived in a two-story house, one of the largest and most attractive houses in town. The front room of Don Augusto's house was a *tienda*. Imported products from the States—Snickers bars, Marlboro cigarettes, and cans of Shasta Iced Tea—lined the shelves behind the front counter. Don Augusto sat on a stool in the corner, smoking.

Don Augusto had been old when Sam lived in San Cristóbal, and if he hadn't aged at all since Sam had last seen him, it was probably because if he aged any more, he'd be dead. Don Augusto peered at him through a screen of cigarette smoke. Sam stuck his hand out and Don Augusto grabbed it with his thin, boney fingers.

He expected Don Augusto to welcome him back to town, hacking his surprise and pleasure. The first words Don Augusto spoke, however, were, "I know. You want your old house back." Don Augusto smiled at him, a grin deficient of teeth.

Sam didn't say anything, and Don Augusto coughed before sticking the cigarette back in his mouth and pulling a long drag from it. "Fortunately, your old house is available."

"Great," Sam said. "But I'll only be needing it for a week."

Don Augusto produced what must have been a laugh, although the sound was more like someone choking. "A week. A year. A lifetime. Okay. A week." He reached into the drawer of a desk and pulled out a pair of keys.

The house was a block from the lake. It was two stories and had a balcony. When he lived here, Sam used to sit at night on his balcony, drinking Gallo beer and listening to the music from the whorehouse next door. Often the whorehouse's windows would be open, and he would have a bird's eye view of the lovemaking below.

He found the house much the same as when he'd lived in it: the large, pine table in the dining room, the three-burner stove in the kitchen, the double bed with its thin, foam mattress (he hoped it had been replaced in the last ten years). On the second floor, he discovered the same pile of rotting boards in the storage room. Whatever project they were going to serve had been abandoned long ago. He stood on the balcony, gazing at the lake, a brilliant blue in the mid-morning sunshine. Smelling the fresh air, he thought, I could live here forever. He knew he'd thought this a hundred times before, in this exact place, and he also knew it had been a fanciful idea, as it was now.

He returned downstairs, calculating what he would need for the next few days: sheets for the bed, toilet paper, food, bottled water. As he headed out to buy the provisions, he felt a touch of doubt. Shouldn't he return to the States immediately?

He walked briskly to the Guatel office, but when he dialed from the pay phone, he heard the same indifferent ringing. He put the phone down and dialed the other number he knew by heart, his mother's. She lived alone in Columbus, Ohio, where she'd been a fourth-grade teacher until she retired. His father had died in a car accident when Sam was fourteen. He'd lost track of his older brother, who'd moved to California when Sam was in college.

His mother answered on the third ring.

"Hi, Mom."

"Sam?"

"How are you?"

"How are *you*? You haven't called me in five months."

"I'm fine."

"Are you sure? You sound like you have a cold."

"It must be the phone. We have a bad connection. I'm in Guatemala."

"Yes, I know."

"You haven't heard from Laura, have you?"

"Who?"

"Laura."

"Laura?" She paused. "Are you all right, honey?"

"I'm fine. How are you?"

"I'm the same, Sam. Living one day at a time. Keeping my nose to the grindstone. All the clichés. Did I tell you Jennifer Adler won the lottery last month? Four and a half million dollars. Can you believe it? Her whole life will be different." She laughed. "Unless it stays the same. Thanks for calling, Sam. I'm going to let you go because I know how expensive a phone call is. Take care of your cold."

"I don't have a cold."

"Say hello to everyone in Guatemala. Say hello to Consuela and the kids."

"How did you know she had kids?" he said, but she'd hung up. His last coin trickled into the slot and disappeared.

After buying what he needed, he ate lunch on the balcony, watching the prostitutes next door hang laundry in the courtyard. He'd made himself his usual Guatemalan lunch, what Peace Corps volunteers used to call *campo* spaghetti: noodles and tomato sauce. He could see the clouds forming over the mountains to the west. Again, he thought: I could live here forever.

After doing the dishes, he combed his hair and walked outside. He had planned to stroll around town and renew acquaintances with the people he'd spent time with ten years ago, but everyone he saw in the doorways of *tiendas* or leaning out of the front windows of their houses acknowledged him as if they'd seen him every day, with light and cheerful calls of "*Buenas tardes*, Don Samuel!"

He soon found himself within half a block of the shoe factory. The guard at the front gate greeted him as if he were expected and waved him into the building. Consuela was in a corner office on the first floor, sitting at a desk piled with papers. She looked up at him and smiled, her teeth brilliant white. When she stood up, he kissed her on the cheek. She laughed. "This is your daytime kiss. Very proper." He put his arm around her waist and tried to pull her toward him in a more passionate display, but she freed herself, laughing again. "No," she said. "You were right the first time. The day is for business." She pointed to her desk. "We have many orders from around the country, even some from Honduras and El Salvador."

She smiled at him. "Would you like to help?"

They worked until well past dusk. Afterwards, he ate dinner at her house again—her mother made *frijoles* with eggs, plantains, and tortillas—and when they were finished, they walked by the lake. The night was brilliant and warm, and they could see the moon and stars reflected in the smooth, black water. They stepped into a grove of pine trees and kissed. This was the first time he'd cheated on his wife, although he rationalized it this way: Consuela was someone he had known before he was married, and if he kissed her now it was only because he hadn't kissed her enough when he was her boyfriend. She even let him touch her breasts, and he was thrilled with the soft roundness of them.

When the moon disappeared behind a cloud, Consuela said, "It's late. We have to work tomorrow."

Early in the morning, Sam returned to the Guatel office. He put his coins in the slot above the phone and dialed. When the phone at his house rang, he listened, expectant. Someone answered—a woman—but it wasn't Laura. The unexpected voice confused him, and he hung up.

Walking away from the phone, he thought the voice sounded like Laura's mother's. This reassured him. Diane probably had come to stay with Laura in order to comfort her about his disappearance.

I'll stay another day here, he thought, only another day.

After work—Consuela had put him in charge of the out-of-country shoe accounts—and after dinner, he sat with Consuela by the lake. They kissed passionately, and he knew Consuela had the most tender lips he'd ever kissed.

In the pause between kisses, he asked about her children. She giggled and kissed him again. "They are good boys," she said.

"Yes," he said, "but I'm wondering who . . . who is their . . . ?"

He stopped speaking when he saw something faintly troubling pass over Consuela's face, something like disappointment and fear. Quickly, however, it was gone, replaced by her bright smile. She kissed him again and said, "Where have you been?"

He knew he should say something about his wife and children, but he feared the consequences of his revelation. It was one thing to wear a wedding ring, it was another to confess his status outright. He thought she would leave him instantly. He wanted to linger with his past, to hold on to it as long as he could—even if it was only for one more night. He said, "I've been in my country."

"Yes," she said. "And it must have been nice to visit." She paused to open the buttons of her blouse. "But this is your country now."

In the morning, he passed by the phone in front of Guatel, and he was only half tempted to walk up to it. He hurried to work, where he joined Consuela in the office overlooking the lake and began to think about where the factory might increase its exports. Before he returned to his wife and daughters, he vowed to find an outlet in the United States willing to sell the shoes made at Consuela's factory. If he left Consuela heartbroken, he thought, he would at least leave her wealthier.

Although the factory had a four-color catalogue of the shoes it manufactured, Sam knew he would have to produce an English-language catalogue. He guessed this would take a week or two, and he was worried this was too much time. Already, Laura might have started up with Charlie. He was, no doubt, consoling her even now.

The factory had a room with its marketing materials, and Sam pulled a catalogue from one of the shelves. Next to the shelf, he noticed an unopened box—on the address label was his name. He looked around, thinking someone might have played a joke on him. But he was the only person in the room. When he opened the box, he discovered a hundred or more shoe catalogues—all in English. Again, he looked around, prepared for someone to spring from one of the dusty corners, laughing. He had an eerie sensation of *déjà vu*. At the same time, he wondered what dark trick was being played on him.

He walked to the single, small window in the room and looked out across San Cristóbal. On a hillside in the distance, he could see the *calvario*, the temple where he and Consuela used to go to escape the curious eyes of the town. Behind the *calvario* was a two-story house, painted celestial blue. They used to talk, half jokingly, about moving into the house when they were married.

He knew the *calvario* and the house, knew them well, but he also thought he knew this view, framed by the small window.

But I've never been here, he told himself.

He left the storage room and found Consuela at her desk. He explained how he'd planned to design brochures in English and how, minutes later, he'd discovered them in the marketing room in a box with his name on it.

"Magic," Consuela said, and when this didn't satisfy him, she sighed. "Perhaps they are here," she said, "because I was hoping you would return."

He was struck by the look in her eyes—plaintive, tender.

"I love you," he said, surprised at how easily the words left his lips.

On Sunday, Sam decided to take Consuela and her two sons on a picnic. He rented a canoe from Don Hector, who lived in an adobe house near the lake. When Sam suggested the two boys wear lifejackets, they frowned. "We know how to swim," said Pablo, the oldest.

"You do?" asked Sam, who'd always been amazed by the number of children living around the lake who couldn't swim. "Who taught you?"

Pablo looked away, smiling, as his brother, César, giggled. "Well?" Sam asked.

"A nice man taught us," Pablo said, and César giggled again.

They drifted toward the middle of the lake, enjoying the sunny day, before Sam directed the canoe toward the shore below the grove of pine trees where he and Consuela had gone the last few nights to kiss, cuddle, and reminisce.

Consuela had packed a lunch of hardboiled eggs, sodas, and jalapeño chips, and they ate it quickly. Consuela dozed under the shade of a pine tree, but Sam was restless, so he suggested a game to the boys, although he didn't know what they could play.

"Frisbee," suggested Pablo, and César pulled a disc from Consuela's bag.

The disc wasn't the cheap, thin kind sold in Guatemala. It was a Wham-O, 175-gram, World Class frisbee. Sam wondered whether he had brought it with him when he was a Peace Corps volunteer, but the only sports equipment he remembered having was a pair of baseball gloves. They'd been ruined when he left them on his porch in the rain.

Pablo and César raced toward the shore, spreading out on the wide, sandy surface. "To me!" César cried. "To me, *Papá*!"

Sam had started his throw before he registered what César had said. He stopped, the frisbee falling from his grip. He wondered if this was how César saw him now, as a father figure. He felt a measure of pride but also a stab of fear—he would only disappoint the boy when he left.

Later, after dinner and after Pablo and César had gone to bed, Sam and Consuela sat under the same pine tree they had earlier. Neither made a move to kiss each other. Sam felt the beginning of something returning to him, like the tide, slow and inevitable, although he didn't know precisely what it was. A memory, he guessed.

"Are you tired of this?" he asked.

"Of what?" she replied.

He didn't know exactly. He'd only been reaching, hoping she would add what was missing.

"I had a girlfriend in college," he said. "Her name was Laura. We talked about getting married. But I wanted to join the Peace

Corps. She wasn't as adventurous, but she said she would wait for me."

Consuela sighed as if she'd heard the story before, but he saw she was listening. Her eyes, bright under the moonlight that sliced through the pine trees, looked up at him. "In college, I had a friend named Charlie. He liked Laura, too. He always told me that if I didn't marry Laura, he would."

He paused. "I know Laura liked Charlie, liked him a lot, but she loved me. And I loved her, too, I guess."

"Did she wait for you when you were in the Peace Corps?" Consuela asked.

"Yes, she did. Yes, but I . . . ." He'd dated Consuela without telling Laura. He'd rationalized it this way: once he left Guatemala, he'd never see Consuela again. This part of his history, his history in Guatemala, his history with Consuela, would be a detour, a pleasant side trip, and he would return to Laura and pick up his old life where he'd left it.

"Maybe it was arrogant on my part, but I felt I knew what my life would be like with Laura," he told Consuela. "I could see it clearly—five, ten, twenty years ahead of me—I could see it all. At least, I thought I could. It would be a good life—predictable, but good. I could even see the time I'd take Laura back to Guatemala because she'd want to see the country. But I wouldn't bring her here, to San Cristóbal. I couldn't."

"Why?" Consuela asked.

Because, he wanted to say, you would be here, and if I saw you, I'd want you again. And I'd always wonder what my life would have been like with you.

Now he wanted to kiss Consuela—to kiss her and more— but he knew it was time to go home, if it wasn't too late.

Consuela put her hands on the back of his neck and pulled his head toward her breasts. He smelled her, a familiar smell of pine needles, of the lake. In her warmth, he felt soothed and settled, almost at home.

"It'll be over soon," she said.

On Monday, he woke early to go to the phone at Guatel. He called his and Laura's number and her mother answered, sounding chipper. She'd been awake for hours, he supposed. He'd always half admired, half dreaded her energy. He saw it in Laura, too: someone who burned steadily on high temperatures, with a seemingly endless amount of fuel. He had always imagined that Laura would outlive him by ten or even twenty years, a happy widow, someone to brighten up an old age home well into her nineties.

"It's Sam," he said. "Sam Madison."

"Sam! Hello! This is unexpected. How are you?"

"I'm . . . ." He stopped. "I'm calling to ask you . . . ." He stopped again,

"Sam, are you all right? Are you having one of your . . ."

He interrupted: "How's Laura?"

"Laura's fine," she said. "The two girls are fine. They're the same, just as you'd expect. I thought I gave you her and Charlie's new phone number the last time we spoke."

"Yes. You . . ."

"Laura said she sent you a Christmas card with a photo of the girls. Did you get it?"

"Yes," he said, realizing now what had set off his latest episode and remembering, as he always did at this juncture, the long-ago plunge over the waterfall and waking up in a hospital to find Consuela above him, concerned, relieved. "It arrived a few days ago."

"Better late than never. They're beautiful girls, aren't they?" She didn't wait for a response. "You shouldn't hesitate to call Laura."

"I'd like to," he said. "If I could convince myself . . . I mean, sometimes I think I made a mistake in not . . ."

"A mistake?" Diane said. "Who doesn't make mistakes? We could live a mistake-free life only if we had ten lives to experiment with. Listen, Laura forgave you a long time ago. It's water under the bridge—or over the falls, I should say. Oh, how crass. I'm sorry, Sam. Please, you take care of yourself. I'll tell Laura you called."

She hung up before he could answer.

Late in the afternoon at the shoe factory, Consuela found him at his desk, writing letters to shoe stores in the United States. "I want to finish these before I leave," he said.

"Leave?" she asked, her brow wrinkled in concern. "Where are you going?"

"Home," he said.

She remained in his office, sitting in a corner chair, looking worriedly at him.

When dusk fell and the factory workers had left, when the only people who remained in the building were the two of them and a night guard, she asked him if he was finished.

"Last letter," he said, holding it up before placing it in the envelope and sealing it.

"Done," he said. "Is your mother making dinner?"

Consuela nodded.

"It'll be my last meal at your parents' house."

"What do you mean?" she said.

"Because I'll be going home."

"Home?" Her voice was tight, tense.

The only light on in the office was the light above his desk, and it wasn't strong. But it was powerful enough to let him see her, her long black hair and cheeks that, after ten years, remained glowing and youthful.

"Home," he said. He took her hand and kissed it. "With you. I'm sorry, Consuela. It happened again, didn't it?"

Consuela nodded. "You went away again—a long way away."

"I always come back." He cupped her hands in his hands. "And I always want to come back." He lifted her left hand in front of his eyes. "Will you wear your ring again?"

"It's here," she said, and she pulled a gold ring, a ring to match his, from her pocket and slipped it on her finger.

He didn't want to wait until they had returned to their blue house above the *calvario*. He wanted her now, here, with the smell of shoe dye wafting from below. It was a heavy, sweet smell, one which would now become mixed with the smell of her, the smell of their love. Touching her, kissing her, he let the smells fill him. He hoped they would find, this time, a place in him deeper than doubt, more profound than regret.

That was. This is. And this is enough. Yes, yes it is.

Defending The Woman

Pablo kicks aside an empty can before he reaches the bodies. The three guerrillas—two men and a woman—have just finished lunch, some sort of rice and tomato paste dish it appears, given what is left in the small pot beside the smoldering ash. The meal seems unappetizing and unlike what he has come to expect of guerrillas. He has always known guerrillas to eat what he eats: beans, scrambled eggs, tortillas. He is disturbed by the thought that rice and tomato paste has been their last meal. He cannot imagine that they enjoyed it, although he can see how the meal might have become necessary. Having days before eaten what was good—beans, eggs, tortillas—the guerrillas were left with tomato paste and rice. After they settled in a patch of high grass, the only cover in an endless cow pasture, the woman probably improvised the meal, exaggerating its appeal in order to calm the men's complaints. Her cooking must have been good, or their hunger great, because they'd eaten nearly all of what had been in the pot. They were probably exchanging "*Buen provechos*"—or whatever the after-meal saying was in their language—when he pulled the trigger.

The woman's hair is spread in the ash—it is hard to tell where her hair ends and the ash begins. She lies face down, and Pablo is grateful that she has fallen that way. He shot her through the ear, and he doesn't want to see what the bullet has made of her face.

Pablo's partner is talking. He has probably been talking the whole time. Now he is saying that it is too bad the woman isn't still alive because they might have had some fun with her.

These are, Pablo knows, the first deaths his partner, only a boy, has seen, and he is not taking it well. But then, he has never known anyone to take it well. There are two types of reactions. The first is the kind the boy is showing, excessive talking, usually as compensation for an earlier failure to act. (Pablo and his partner had spotted the guerrillas from a distance—a rifle point sticking out from the high grass had convinced them that the smoke was not from a mere *vaquero's* lunch—and had crept up on them with the quick stillness of snakes, but after a whispered countdown, only Pablo fired). The other reaction is silence, a numbness in the face of what has been committed. Silence is, by far, the more troubling response.

Pablo is glad that his latest partner is verbal. Nevertheless, he wants to tell the boy to be quiet. The woman is dead, after all, and she deserves reverence because she is a woman and has cooked. He looks at the boy but says nothing. The boy continues to talk while they wait for the lieutenant, whom Pablo has radioed.

He stares again at the woman. It is not unusual, a woman guerrilla, but she is the first he has seen. He knows from the conversations of other soldiers that most women guerrillas work as doctors and nurses. The woman he killed, however, was a regular guerrilla, although, it seemed, an insecure one. Whereas the two men put down their AK-47 assault rifles during the meal, the woman kept hers slung across her shoulder. It was her rifle point, then, that he had noticed sticking up from the long grass.

Like him, she is *indígena*—he can tell by the color of her skin and the absence of hair on her arms, which are spread around the fire as if she is about to embrace it. Most guerrillas are *indígenas*, he knows, enticed to join the cause after hearing promises of paradise, a land free of repressive generals and tyrannical landowners. Most of the army's soldiers are also *indígenas*, boys seized from corn fields and cattle pastures.

Pablo hears the lieutenant's jeep and turns to see it roll over the field in excited bounces. Three soldiers accompany the lieutenant, and when the jeep stops, the soldiers jump out and march briskly in different directions, securing the field. The lieutenant orders the talkative boy to guard the rear, and the boy runs in the direction in which the jeep has come.

"Tell me what happened," the lieutenant says.

Pablo tells the lieutenant the story. He tells it briefly, and when he is finished, he hears a song. The lieutenant has left the jeep running, with its radio on, and the song fills the desolate field with jubilant notes. Pablo knows the song. It is by The Woman.

When Pablo first heard a song by The Woman, he was not yet old enough to work on the coffee *finca* like his father and older brother, Juan, but he did on occasion accompany his father, who picked coffee beans with the speed and precision of a hummingbird pinching spiders from their webs. His father worked beside a man who brought his radio to the coffee fields. The radio was good. On certain days it picked up a station from the capital that played music from the United States.

One day Pablo heard a song that attracted him like a light, and he left his father in order to stand beside the radio. The song began with a rhythmic rattling and, as if above it, like a swarm of bees, a buzzing sound. Another instrument, making a sound like rain falling, joined in, and then, most compelling and beautiful, came her voice.

Pablo didn't understand the words she sang, but he was not accustomed to understanding what was said and sung on the radio. He spoke hardly any Spanish and there had never been any songs on the radio in Pokomchí, the *indígena* language spoken in his village. He learned the singer's name was The Woman, however, because when the song was over, the disc jockey repeated it five times, shouting it as if he were announcing a winning lottery number or a soccer goal.

In January, his father permitted Pablo to go to school. At eleven years old, he was not the oldest boy in his first-grade class in the one-room cement schoolhouse in the village. Esteban, who had a faint dab of hair above his lips, had recently celebrated his twelfth birthday. Pablo and Esteban became friends, although their friendship was not free from competitiveness. They were always on opposing teams in the soccer games played after school, and frequently during these games they would collide in pursuit of the ball and, inevitably, fight.

Pablo was smarter than Esteban. He learned Spanish quicker and frequently translated for Esteban because their teacher, a broad-chested *ladino* with a square head, spoke no Pokomchí. Esteban, however, had an easier time with girls and talked about them casually and confidently, as if they were as common and workable as soil and not elusive creatures who knew secrets and possessed treasures.

By the time Pablo and Esteban were in fourth grade, their teacher no longer arrived every day with the energy it took to teach six grades simultaneously. Frequently, he indulged in what the students called "cigarette days." On these days, the teacher would sit on his desk and stare out the window, smoking one cigarette after the other while the students entertained themselves however they could. Usually the boys played soccer and the girls watched or drifted home.

During one of his "cigarette days," the teacher turned on the radio he had brought to school. The radio was tuned to a station from Cobán, the large town to the north. "Dance," the teacher said when a song played. "You know how to dance, don't you?"

He ordered everyone to push their desks to the side of the room. "There," he said. "There's room to dance."

Esteban walked across the room and took Gloria's hand. Gloria, a tall girl, wore a bright red *güipil*, which didn't hide her large chest. Waiting for the next song, Esteban and Gloria stood in the center of the room, as solemn as a couple at the altar.

The radio played the song by The Woman that Pablo had first heard in the coffee field. As he watched Esteban dance with Gloria, the two of them rocking back and forth as if they were on horseback, the music transported him, as if he were dancing, too, but dancing in the sky. Esteban may have been in love with Gloria, but Pablo was in love with The Woman, and The Woman was his. He had, after all, discovered her, claimed her long ago.

"*Re' wili re'* The Woman," he told Esteban as they walked home after school.

"*Chajari?*" Esteban said.

"That was The Woman, the song you danced to."

"The song's called The Woman?"

"No, the singer."

"How do you know?"

"I've heard it before. She's American." Pablo spoke as if he knew her.

Esteban preferred to talk about his own triumphs. "What do you think of Gloria?" he asked.

"She's all right," Pablo said, although in truth he thought she was very pretty.

"Yesterday she let me hold her breasts," Esteban said. "They're very big breasts."

"The Woman also has very big breasts," he said, unwilling to allow Esteban his victory.

"How do you know?"

"Because I saw her two weeks ago in Cobán. I was with my father. He was buying fertilizer. She was giving a concert."

"Liar."

"I didn't go to the concert. But I saw her beforehand. She was shopping in the market."

"Did she say anything to you?"

"She asked me what my name was."

"Liar. I bet The Woman doesn't even speak Spanish."

"I don't know. She spoke to me in Pokomchí."

Esteban looked at him suspiciously. "Are you sure?"

When Pablo was in the fifth grade, his father inherited the radio from the man he worked with in the coffee fields after he dropped dead one afternoon. Late at night, Pablo would remain awake, the radio pressed to his ear, listening to songs from the capital. One night the disc jockey's voice was louder and more dramatic than usual, and it had every right to be because the news he announced was significant: "This is . . . this is . . . this is the latest song from The Woman!"

The next afternoon on their walk home, Esteban told Pablo that he had touched Florinda's pubic hair. Florinda was a plump girl with a big smile. "It felt just like grass," Esteban said, grinning.

Pablo grinned back. "I got a telegram from The Woman."

"Who?"

"The Woman, the American singer."

"Liar."

"It's true."

Esteban didn't speak for a while. "What'd it say?" he asked.

"She said she has a new song, and it'll be coming to the radio station in Cobán."

And it did come, quicker than Pablo expected, filling the schoolhouse the next month. The song sounded like a thousand heartbeats. As it played, Esteban danced with Florinda, bouncing his hip off hers. Some of the other students joined in, shyly shaking.

When the song finished, Esteban found Pablo in a corner of the room, next to an open window, and shook him by the shoulder. "You were right," Esteban said with wonder. "You were right about The Woman!"

That year, half a dozen songs by The Woman played regularly on the Cobán radio station, and The Woman became famous in Pablo's village.

When school started the following January, the students from the village were told they would have to take classes in the elementary school in Santa Cruz, the nearby town, because the government was closing most rural schools.

Pablo became popular with his new classmates in part because of his invented acquaintance with The Woman. Not everyone believed he was The Woman's friend, but they never doubted his understanding of her music. To anyone who was curious, he would explain, with patient exactitude, the meaning of each of her songs. He had always associated her music and unintelligible words with certain images, and in time those images settled into his mind with the indelibility of a recurring dream. With righteous certainty, he described those images—exotic towns filled with fast cars, lonely men worshipping at the feet of long-haired, generous women—and his classmates could only nod in wonder.

Esteban was still his best friend. They walked home together at the end of each school day in a ragged line with other students from their village. But Esteban always seemed preoccupied, depressed even. Esteban had grown taller and heftier over the years, but no handsomer and no smarter, and in the school in Santa Cruz he did not enjoy the same success with girls. There were too many handsome boys from town who interested the girls from the village. And the town girls, even the *indígena* town girls, thought themselves too good for the likes of Esteban, who still could hardly speak Spanish.

When Esteban complained to him, Pablo listened attentively, but he didn't share Esteban's loneliness. And he did not speak with longing, as Esteban did, of their village schoolhouse and former teacher.

A month after school started, Pablo was elected class treasurer. After he made his required speech at the front of the classroom, everyone applauded, and two girls in the front row hummed the first few notes of the most recent song by The Woman. María Elena, their teacher, smiled at him.

Grinning, Pablo returned to his seat. From the desk next to his, Esteban whispered, "Your girlfriend's a whore."

"What?"

"The Woman, she's a whore."

"What are you saying?"

"Look."

Esteban handed him the day's *El Grafico*, a newspaper from the capital that a boy sold around town on his bike. Esteban often bullied the boy into giving him a paper because he liked to look at the scantily clad women in the entertainment pages. Today's paper contained a photograph of The Woman standing in a grove of cherry trees, her breasts and waist censored with black blocks. The caption said The Woman had just published a collection of photographs called *All of The Woman*.

Pablo stared hard at the photograph. He had never seen a picture of The Woman, had never even imagined what she looked like, despite saying to Esteban long ago that she had large breasts. When he thought of her, it wasn't as *this*. He felt betrayed. He wanted to say, "That isn't her."

"Whore," Esteban said.

"Shut up, Esteban," Pablo said, throwing the paper back at him.

But Esteban continued: "The Woman's a whore, The Woman's a whore."

Their classmates were listening now. With an audience, Pablo couldn't back down. He shoved Esteban. Esteban responded, standing and punching him on the shoulder. Pablo stood and returned the punch. The two of them half hugged and half wrestled, as they used to do during soccer games, until María Elena screamed, "Stop!" They did stop, swiftly repentant. But María Elena, following school rules, sent them home.

They were walking back to the village on the logging road when two soldiers sprang from behind a tree and ordered them to lie on their stomachs. After the soldiers told them what to do, Pablo and Esteban stood and marched in front of the soldiers, their backs receiving an occasional poke from a rifle point. A truck, covered with an olive-colored canvas, was waiting on the other side of the hill.

Pablo and Esteban were soldiers.

Pablo is a soldier, standing beside the lieutenant, who tells him to search the guerrillas. On the two dead men, he finds identification. The woman, however, has only a card in her pocket, a Valentine's card, although Valentine's Day has long passed. The card isn't addressed to anyone. It has a pre-printed message and below it, a signature in an illegible hand. Pablo hands the card to the lieutenant.

"Looks like the bitch doesn't have a name," the lieutenant says.

Pablo says nothing. He was once a talker at deaths, but now he is the opposite. He says nothing but thinks about how he defended The Woman and how his defending her led him, by and by, to this spot.

He looks at the dark skin of her arms, he looks at the spread of her black hair. He can't say she is a stranger now. *Sister*, he thinks, crouching as in prayer. *Sister, I . . . Sister, forgive me, sister . . . .*

But just as quickly, he is standing above her again, and he steps back so his boots no longer touch the ends of her hair.

He doesn't look at her anymore. Instead, he follows the music, and it takes him beyond the pasture to the mountains in the distance and the clouds hugging them like shawls. Above the clouds is an expanse of blue. The music carries him here and leaves him half swimming, half floating across the sky.

For the first time since he'd met her three years before, she seemed like a stranger. Perhaps it was the regular, rhythmic nature of her lovemaking that allowed him to distance himself from her, view her with curious detachment, as if he were watching an exercise video. Diane had never been predictable in her movements and ways. Terry always had felt connected to her spontaneity—the swift, impulsive decisions she made at the training center—and her herky-jerky carriage, how she always wobbled slightly, as if in need of crutches. He'd even found something compelling about her kaleidoscope face, the malleable cheeks and chin that could turn her in an instant from a sour, mean-spirited woman into a cheery and even pretty one.

Only now, in bed, had he found her predictable, like a clock or workday, and although she was naked, he saw her as he remembered seeing her the first time: a woman a few steps past her prime with hair bleached from too much sunlight, her face splotched from too much alcohol and the smell of cigarettes hanging around her.

Diane stopped suddenly, allowing her weight to rest on him. The break in her rhythm brought Terry back from his reverie. He felt the flesh on her hips, saw, in the mirror behind her, the large, dark freckles on her back.

"Is something wrong?" she asked, wiping his sweaty hair from his forehead. "Are you thinking about your wife?"

It was like her to ask him about Paulina, to be indiscreet in the midst of indiscretion. He knew her again, familiar in her strangeness, predictable in her unpredictability.

"No," he said, although now he was.

When they'd finished, Diane stroked his hair, blond and thinning around the crown and temples. He was thirty-five, although every Guatemalan he knew thought he was at least forty. It was one of the many ironies he'd found in the country: middle-aged men looked like teenagers but the majority died before they reached sixty, victims of murder, accidents, disease or alcohol abuse.

"I thought I'd lost you there for a second," Diane said. "I thought for sure you were feeling guilty." She took a drag on her cigarette and released the smoke above them. "And you probably should feel guilty."

"Thanks," Terry said, irritated. He was tempted to grab her cigarette and take a puff, although he hadn't smoked since he was seventeen.

"And I should feel guilty too," she said. "Less guilty than you—you're the married one here. But guilty because your wife's a nice, attractive woman and I'm an old, desperate one."

Terry wondered if she expected him to protest this description. Most women would have, he supposed, but Diane probably wouldn't. He had always been impressed with her ability to see things as they were.

"But I have to say," she added, "I'm glad we did it, even if you hate yourself for the next two weeks or two years. If we hadn't, I'd be thinking about it for months, imagining what it would have been like."

Terry wanted to think of something witty to say in return. He would have, he knew, if they had been at work, where they had used banter to combat the sexual tension between them. Now, however, his mind was empty of jokes. She was right: he did feel guilty. He would probably feel even guiltier when he left her house, which he would need to do soon. Paulina would be expecting him.

They would have to resolve this quickly, come to an agreement about how they would treat it. The facts were these: having heard they had lost the bid on the new USAID contract, Terry and Diane had gone to her house to console each other over drinks. They'd never had the drinks. Instead, they'd gone straight to her bedroom, with the slim mirror on the far wall and photographs of jaguars and monkeys above the headboard. They hadn't spoken about what they were going to do before jumping in their cars to drive to her house or even after they'd stepped into the hallway. It had been understood, although exactly how, he didn't know.

But what did it mean? He didn't think she'd expect anything else from him. She would be fine with allowing this to be a one-time affair. They had worked together for three years and now, because they'd lost the contract, they probably wouldn't work together again. Diane would go back to the States, where World Rock International would give her a desk job, and he would stay in Guatemala with his wife and son.

Her hand was on his penis, stiff and resting against her thigh, which was damp with sweat and semen.

"You trying to tell me something?" she asked, and before he could answer, she'd slipped him inside her. They were on their sides, face to face, and he guessed she expected him to take control this time. He had a moment of paralysis, however, thinking of his wife. It was one thing, he thought, to have sex in a flight of misguided sorrow, but a second time could only be calculated. He didn't know how he could explain this objection to Diane, and he didn't try. He allowed her to pull him on top of her, and he began to move with the same rhythm she'd employed. After a minute, he thought he would go flaccid, dulled by his own dullness. But, again, she surprised him. She had been following his rhythm, keeping time with her own movements, but suddenly she became motionless beneath him. He slowed down and was about to ask her if anything was wrong when she smiled—her smile always improved her looks, hiding her wrinkles and giving her eyes a certain brightness—and said, "Is this the way your wife was on your wedding night? Doing her duty?"

It wasn't—not exactly. Although a virgin, and definitely afraid of sex, his wife had attempted to be interested in what they were doing. She hadn't exactly moved beneath him, but kind of trembled. She'd reached awkwardly at his back and had once, as if by accident, brushed his ass with her hand, which she'd moved back to his shoulder. It had been over quickly, and they were both relieved.

The memory depressed him, and it embarrassed him to think Diane had conjured up an accurate picture of him and his wife in their wide, soft bed in Hotel El Dorado.

"She tried," he said.

"What?" Diane asked. "Moaned a little?" And Diane moaned like a bad actress, humming a loud "mmm."

He was too defeated to tell her she was right. Giving up, he lay on top of her and closed his eyes.

"I'm sorry," she said, stroking his neck. "I was only teasing."

Terry had never been a good liar, probably because he'd always been forgiven everything he'd done. He'd never done anything as grave, however, as cheating on his wife.

Opening the door of his ranch-style house behind a high, brick fence in *zona diez* in Guatemala City, he half expected Paulina to have packed his bags and lined them up in the living room. But the house was the same, and he was relieved. She hadn't discovered his infidelity by telepathy, read his guilt from kilometers away, although he wouldn't have put it past her. She had powers others didn't—she could predict earth tremors hours ahead of time and was better than any meteorologist at forecasting rain. When their son was a baby, she would wake up in the middle of the night minutes before he began howling from the pain of his colic. And one time, when Marco was three and they were vacationing in Livingston, she had sprung from the hotel bed at two in the morning and found him inches from the edge of the swimming pool, about to toddle in.

Her sense of the natural world didn't extend to herself, however. She didn't know from one month to the next when her period was due, and therefore was reluctant to practice the rhythm method. Instead, he wore condoms on the occasions he could interest her in sex. He'd even had Diane speak to her about a diaphragm, but Paulina frowned at the idea.

"Good evening," she called from the kitchen, where she was making dinner. Despite years of English in high school and close to a year during her brief try at college, she was far from fluent and had a pronounced accent. Even with her light skin, she could never pass as a *norteamericana*.

"Hi," he answered, and moved from the hallway to the living room, where Marco was sitting in front of the TV, watching a talk show. Terry marched to the set and turned it off. "Homework?" he asked his son, whose skin was darker than Paulina's, almost as dark as his grandfather's.

Marco shrugged and said, "*No la tengo*."

"In English," his father said. This was a rule he and Paulina tried to employ: in the house, only English was to be spoken, although he suspected Paulina broke the rule when she was alone with their son. Marco was attending what was supposed to be a bilingual elementary school; however, only one of the seven teachers was a native English speaker. Home was the best place for Marco to learn, but Terry found him a reluctant student, sticking with Spanish when he could, which was more and more often, since over the last several weeks Terry usually showed up at home tired and distracted.

"OK," Terry said, waving his hand. "If you don't have homework, you should read a book or play basketball. Goddamn TV. It's an international pest." He mumbled the last few words.

"All right, Dad," the boy said. "I play basketball now."

Terry didn't know if there was time to play before dinner, but his son was trying to cooperate—he had even spoken in English, although it pained Terry that Marco wasn't fluent. Marco ran into his room off the living room and emerged with a basketball. "When will I have dinner?" he asked.

"Half an hour," Terry said. "Come back in half an hour."

"*Bueno, regreso,*" Marco said, and Terry didn't know if these Spanish words were accidental or a taunt, but the boy was gone. Terry could hear him outside, pounding the ball on the brick walkway leading to the gate.

He meandered to the kitchen, where his wife was piling beefsteak onto a long plate. The kitchen was half clouded in smoke. He stooped and kissed his wife on the forehead. She was nearly nine inches shorter than he, and she had begun to look like most Guatemalan women, her weight settling into her waist. Although he knew this would happen to her when he married her, the thought of it disturbed him lately.

She said in Spanish, "You have been using a rose-scented soap." She did not say it as a question, although he knew it was, and he was prepared. Before leaving Diane's, he had showered, and he'd been unhappy to discover she had only a single bar of perfumed soap. He'd thought of only rinsing off, but he concluded this was a more risky path. Afterwards, to his wife's discerning nose, he might still smell of sex. He gave her his formulated excuse: "We lost the contract today. We thought we'd win, and we had bought beer and wine to celebrate, and when we discovered we'd lost, we drank anyway. Someone dumped beer all over my hair and I wanted to wash it before I came home, so I took a shower at the training center. Rosa, one of the Spanish teachers, leant me a bar of soap."

His long speech sounded rehearsed, and he knew he'd miscalculated. She would suspect he was lying, and would keep this information like a secret and spring it on him in a week or two, asking him again how he came to smell like roses. He would have to remember all the details of his lie—beer on his hair, not rum on his clothes. The soap was Rosa's, not Maria's or Blanca's. If he faltered in a detail, she would know.

"Please, sit down," she said, and called: "Marco!"

"He's playing basketball."

"I told him dinner would be ready soon."

"I sent him to play basketball. He watches too much TV. He's seven years old, he should be outside playing."

Paulina ran a hand through her long, black hair. She had wanted to cut it short the way she'd seen women do in the Mexican soap operas she liked to watch on the days she didn't work, but had left it long to please him. He liked her hair, liked touching it, liked the way it smelled at night, holding the scent of whatever she'd cooked. It had been her hair he'd fallen in love with ten years before when he was a Peace Corps volunteer. She was behind the counter in her father's *agropecuaria*, and he'd asked if she had carrot seeds. He'd come the next month from his site in Chiquimula, three hours away, asking about pesticides, and he'd done more: he'd asked her to lunch. They'd talked about farming and her father, who planned to open stores across the country. They'd talked about music and the United States. What he had found most refreshing about her was her attitude toward the U.S. Unlike most Guatemalans he knew, she had no interest in visiting the States, much less living there. She'd had an uncle who'd gone *mojado* to Chicago and had been beaten up by a pair of white men who'd accused him and a friend of stealing their jobs and had returned home with a broken jaw and a horrible impression of *norteamericanos*.

He saw her twice a month, commuting to the capital and staying in cheap hotels in *zona uno*, treating her to meals and movies. In the theaters, they made out like teenagers. He extended for a third year in the Peace Corps, at the end of which he married her. He hadn't thought to question too deeply his motivation or state of mind. He had grown comfortable in Guatemala, enjoying life's easy pace, more tranquil even than what he'd known as a boy growing up in Canton, Ohio. The only word of caution came from his older brother, who'd once been engaged to a Japanese woman while he was working in Tokyo as an English teacher. At the end of his congratulatory letter, his brother asked, "Are you lonely?"

When his brother, two sisters, and parents showed up to see him married in the Catholic church near the National Palace, they had seemed like tourists—pale, awkward, and more than a little silly with their Spanish learned lazily from Berlitz tapes. He hadn't been unhappy to see them go. During the last few years, however, he had begun corresponding regularly with his brother, who had moved back to Canton to take a job with Goodyear and was dating—seriously, he claimed—a woman from town. He told Terry he could expect to receive a wedding invitation sometime in the next year.

Terry sat with his wife in the dining room, the plates on the table. Terry had bought the place mats in the market in Chichicastenango. They were blue and white, with figures of red deer. His wife had objected to the purchase, preferring the imported household wares sold in department stores in the capital. "They're made in your country," he said. "You should be supporting your fellow Guatemalans."

Paulina may have been patriotic, but not when it came to shopping. She had shrugged and said, "They'll fall apart in six months." They hadn't, and it had been a year, although the color had drained from them, leaving only a pale hint of the original blue.

Sitting across from his wife, looking at his empty plate, he observed her out of the corner of his eyes, saw the shine of her oval face and the glow of her cinnamon-colored eyes. Nervously, he pinched the end of his place mat between his thumb and index finger. He knew what they would discuss, and he wasn't looking forward to it.

"What will you do now, about work?"

She spoke gently, if not, however, without obvious concern. From time to time over the past three months, they had talked about what they would do if World Rock lost the contract, and she was adamant that he should work for her father, who now owned three *agropecuarias* in the capital and others in

Quetzaltenango and Escuintla. Paulina's father needed someone who spoke fluent English and could negotiate the purchase of products from the States, and Terry knew enough about Guatemalan agriculture—he had worked as a crop extentionist as a Peace Corps volunteer—to do the job well. In the past, however, their discussions had been theoretical, and he had never put much passion into them because he thought World Rock would win the contract.

"I was thinking . . . ," he began, and blushed. It was Diane who had suggested he consider a job in the States with World Rock. She was well-liked and well-connected in the organization and could all but guarantee him a position. She had mentioned this before they'd stepped into their cars to drive to her apartment.

"I was thinking I might consider a job in the States," he said. Paulina frowned and opened her mouth, no doubt about to object, but he continued, "Marco isn't learning as much English as he should. Living in the States would help him. It wouldn't have to be a long time. We could stay a few years, then move back here."

She said, "You know how I feel about the United States of America." She spoke the last words with emphasis and a scrunched expression, as if she'd bitten a lemon.

"What happened to your uncle in Chicago doesn't happen to everyone," Terry replied. "There are many people from Latin America, many people from Guatemala, living in the States who are happy."

This hadn't been his standard response to her doubts about the States, far from it. On other occasions, he had seconded her impressions, acknowledging the racism and crime in his country, the insane capitalism which compelled both parents to work while their children grew up alone, the drugs young people indulged in. He had been most outspoken early in his relationship with Paulina, when Guatemala had seemed to him like a paradise, and although he had a more complex view of the situation now—Guatemala, he discovered, is as racist as any place on earth and teenagers bent on self-destruction and without the money to buy drugs turn to alcohol instead—he hadn't shared his evolving perspective with Paulina. Rather, he had discussed it with Diane and the other North Americans at the training center, which over the last three years had become the place where Terry had spent most of his time and made all of his friends. The training center was like a U.S. island in the middle of Guatemala, a place where he could speak English, talk about American politics and sports and joke, respectfully, of course, about Guatemalan food and superstitions. If he had become patriotic, it would seem to Paulina like a sudden conversion.

Paulina said, "My father asked about you today. He will pay you well, Terry."

"As much as I was making at the training center?" he asked, although, having discussed this with her, he knew the answer.

"Perhaps more." She sighed. "My father would one day like to give the business to you. To you and me. And we could give it to Marco."

Terry frowned. It wasn't only his future which was being mapped, but his son's as well.

"There are a thousand other kinds of work," Terry said. "What if Marco wants to be a pianist?"

What if he, Terry, wanted to move back to Canton and become a farmer? What if he wanted to become the curator of the Pro Football Hall of Fame? What if he wanted an American family?

Over the last three years, he'd had enough contact with other Americans to feel satisfied. Now, with his job about to end, he felt at risk of sinking anonymously into his adopted country, with its laughable, secondhand busses from the States, ponderous service in restaurants and colorful trickles of trash on the sides of highways.

"My father's business is very good," Paulina said. It was a statement that didn't answer the question, not directly, but Terry understood: by nature, Guatemalans were conservative. They preferred to hold on to miserable certainty rather than gamble on a better future.

With the coming night, the light had grown softer in the dining room, and from across the table, Paulina seemed far away. He wondered what his life might have been like if he hadn't met her in her father's *agropecuaria*, if, instead, he had found the seeds he'd needed at the hardware store in Chiquimula. He missed the journey he hadn't taken.

"We'll talk about it," he said, feeling tired. He wasn't hungry. He closed his eyes, hoping to find relief from the future and the past, but he saw Diane standing at the door of her apartment as he'd left in his car. She hadn't waved, only watched, her hair lit up from the afternoon light. She was the kind of woman his brother would have liked: tall and thin and unafraid to curse or flirt. Terry had tracked her in his rearview mirror, and she had become increasingly smaller but no less inviting.

"I know my father will want to talk to you soon," Paulina said. "Will you please call him?"

He nodded but didn't open his eyes.

When Marco hadn't come home in half an hour, Terry went to look for him. Paulina didn't trust anyone, especially after dark, and now the darkness was nearly complete. She had good reason to fear. More than a few children of wealthy Guatemalans had been kidnapped. Although Terry and Paulina were far from wealthy, Paulina was vigilant about keeping an eye on Marco, and when he hadn't come home, she berated Terry for having allowed him to go outside at such a late hour, then began to pray, a habit Terry found annoying. He had grown up Catholic but had never really believed in the religion and hadn't been to church in years. Nevertheless, Paulina's anxiety made him uneasy, and he told her he would find their son.

He walked to the park three blocks from the house and spotted Marco on the far court, with the eight-foot baskets. He couldn't see that it was Marco but knew from the strained way the boy hoisted shots from off his right shoulder, almost like he was hurling a shot put. The physical awkwardness reminded Terry of Diane, and he felt a mixture of guilt and regret. Marco was of average height by Guatemalan standards, but no doubt would have been one of the shortest boys in a third-grade class in the U.S. He had inherited from Paulina's side of the family not only their dark complexion, but small stature. Terry thought: *If I had married a woman as tall as Diane . . .* , and he had a brief vision of a blond son racing down a basketball court, leaping and jamming the ball into the rim. This, he knew, was foolish. Terry wasn't much over six feet, and he wouldn't be able to produce a giant, no matter how tall the mother.

Terry lingered a minute, watching his son in the dark. His shot may have been awkward, but it was effective. At one point, Marco made six in a row from a distance of at least ten feet. Terry tried to remember the last time he'd played basketball with his son and couldn't.

When Marco missed a shot, Terry called his name, and

the boy turned around. The two faced each other like strangers before Marco dribbled down the court toward his father, who stood under the opposite basket.

"Dinner's ready," Terry said.

"*Bueno.* I'm very hungry."

But before returning to the house, Terry asked his son to pass him the ball. Terry dribbled down the sideline, imagining himself a player in a great contest, a game to decide whether his country triumphed or failed in a futuristic war settled on the basketball court. It was a fantasy from his youth. He switched the ball to his left hand at mid-court, then back to his right as he drove down the middle of the lane, jumped and dunked the ball.

"The champion!" Terry shouted, throwing up his arms to celebrate his imaginary victory.

His son stared at him from the other end. In the dark, Terry couldn't see the expression on Marco's face, but he imagined him puzzled by his father's antics. Growing up, Terry and his brother used to play games of H-O-R-S-E and *21* on the court in their driveway, and the contests had often lasted until their mother said they were keeping the neighbors awake. His brother would have understood his grandstanding.

Slowly, Terry dribbled back to the other end of the court. "Dunk here," his son said, pointing to the near basket. "I didn't see you. Too dark."

Terry smiled, pleased with his son's interest; he'd misjudged Marco's response. He dribbled out to the top of the key, slammed the ball against the cement, caught it in midair and jammed it into the basket with two hands. His son clapped. "Cool," Marco said.

Terry did a few more dunks, including a reverse, then tried to dunk by jumping from the free-throw line. He came up short, and the ball nicked off the rim. By this time, however, his son had found something else to occupy his attention: Paulina, walking across the grass in the dark.

Even walking quickly, she didn't cover much ground. The discrepancy in their strides had been, in her and Terry's first months together, a source of much laughter and playful teasing. Lately, however, he'd come to see this difference as only one of the countless between them.

She stopped at the edge of the court, and in the darkness,

he couldn't see the expression on her face. "Diane called," she said in a neutral voice. Or was it a cold, knowing voice?

He would liked to have seen her eyes, although even then, he might not have been able to guess what she was thinking. He said, "What did she want?"

There was a pause, and Terry thought Diane might have confessed everything. It was possible that she could have gotten drunk after Terry left and felt free to betray their secret. If she had, it would be over between him and Paulina. The thought half thrilled him.

"She would like you to drive her to the airport Sunday."

There was another pause, although shorter.

"She asked me if I minded," Paulina said. "I said, 'Why should I mind?' She said, 'Yes, why should you mind? You are young and I am old.' What did she mean, Terry?"

He heard the pounding of the basketball against the concrete and turned and saw his son at the far end of the court, jumping in an awkward imitation of the way Terry had jumped. His shot bounced off the rim. Terry turned back to his wife.

This was his chance to say good-bye, to reclaim his life against the backdrop of a Guatemalan night and the beat of a basketball. He could tell his wife about the affair. He could tell her he loved Diane. It was true, in a way. He ran a hand through his thinning hair.

"Was she drunk?" he asked her.

"Who?"

"Diane."

"I don't know."

"She's sad because she's leaving Guatemala. She was probably drinking."

Paulina sighed with what seemed to Terry like relief. She would accept this insufficient explanation for now, although in a few days, a week—when Diane had left the country—she would bring it up again, to probe Terry for the truth. Tonight, however, the danger of her discovering what he'd done had passed, and Terry was too much of a coward to resurrect it by continuing the conversation.

Terry turned and called his son, and the three of them walked back to their house in silence.

By the time Terry and Diane reached the airport, there was

no more to say. Or, rather, there was too much to say, and because it hadn't been said days and months earlier, it never would be.

Ignoring the porters, who descended on them with as much vigor as beggars, Terry carried Diane's two suitcases into the terminal. She followed with a backpack slung over her shoulder. With her jeans and T-shirt, she was dressed as casually as a tourist. Her earrings were small, ceramic replicas of cinnamon-colored Guatemalan children, and they hung low and pattered against her cheeks, red from too much sun and too much drinking. She'd been hung over when he'd met her in the morning—she'd stayed up all night, partying with her neighbors during her *despedida*. Guatemalans treated good-byes seriously, marking them with as much outrageousness as they could manage.

After she checked in, she said thank you and told him he was free to go. This was how she'd said it, with mock seriousness, like a detective dismissing a murder suspect: "Thank you, you're free to go." But from her exaggerated cheeriness, Terry guessed she didn't want him to go, and he said, "Let's have some coffee." There was half an hour left before her flight was to be called.

They walked down the stairs, and Diane talked with the women in booths who sold Guatemalan clothing and jewelry and coffee. She asked many questions about the products—who made them, where they were made, how much the people who made them were paid—and Terry realized she was purposely killing time.

She didn't buy anything. She had bought all she needed in Antigua, she'd told him: a worn *güipil*, which she would hang on her wall in the States, the earrings she was wearing, a tablecloth with a Christmas pattern for her parents. She could have bought more, she said, but she wasn't sentimental. When a thing was over, it was over. The fewer reminders, the better.

With ten minutes left, they did order coffee and sat in plastic chairs next to a two-story window where they could watch planes take off. The coffee was too hot, but Terry drank it anyway, glad to have his mouth full so he wouldn't have to talk. The sooner she was gone, the sooner he could accept the choice he'd made and consider it inevitable. He liked this about Guatemalans: they were fatalistic. Nothing was anyone's fault. It was all God's fault. If he stayed in Guatemala the rest of his life, married to a woman he didn't know, raising a son he felt estranged from, it wasn't his fault. It was the way God wanted it.

Diane said, "Every time I get on a plane, I think it's going to crash."

It wasn't what Terry would have expected her to say.

"But, of course, it rarely happens," she said. "I mean, we worry so much about great disasters when it's the little disasters, added up, that kill us." She pushed her coffee aside. She'd hadn't touched it. "Do you know what I mean?"

"I do," he said, and he did.

I am here. Help me. This is what Graham's telegram to Kathy had said. He could have called, but he didn't think he could handle—*aguantar* is how the Guatemalans he knew would have put it—the long lines in Guatel, the waiting, the bad connection.

"What?" Kathy, the Peace Corps nurse, would have said.

"The ferry I was on from Livingston. It capsized."

"You have to speak up. I can't hear you too well."

"The ferry! It capsized!"

"Whose hat size?"

No, he couldn't have handled it, couldn't have *aguantar*-ed it. The telegram was easier. *I am here. Help me.* Then the name of the sea-front hotel in Puerto Barrios where he'd rented a room. Then his name. He would wait for Kathy to come get him.

By that time, his clothes would be dry (he was still wearing his underwear, and shorts, but he'd taken off his shirt and had hung it on the railing) and maybe he'd feel better. Maybe he would have begun to forget the rush of water, the screams, the panic he felt as he swam hard and fast away from the drowning people. Maybe Kathy and whoever came with her—he imagined someone would come with her, it was a five-hour drive from the capital to Puerto Barrios, and she'd need company—maybe they'd scold him, say he should have gotten on a bus and come straight to the capital. At least he could have called. How would he explain not calling?

—I couldn't *aguantar* it, Kathy. Besides, my clothes were soaked.

—But it would have been faster.

—Right. I even had money. The bills were wet. But, yes, I could have paid for a phone call. Or I could have called collect.

But instead I got this room in Hotel Del Norte because I could *aguantar* that. I mean, all I had to say to the woman at the desk was, "How much for a single?" I handed her the money, and the room was mine. Simple. And later, after I'd sat down, dried out a little, I could even ask her to send the telegram.

Sitting on the second-floor porch of Hotel Del Norte, his eyes on both the water and the road, Graham hears voices come in with the wind off the sea. They say exactly what he'd said in his telegram.

I am here. Help me.

I'm on the ferry to Puerto Barrios. Actually, I'm on top of the ferry. The bottom is packed, mostly with women and children. Even the top is almost full. I've got a nice spot, right in front, with a railing large enough to prop my journal on.

I was in Livingston for three days, and I neglected to write in this journal. What did I do in Livingston? Ate robalo—*really tasty fish—at the African House and drank beer. Looked at women. Drank more beer. The trip was good. It cheered me up, even if I didn't get lucky, only drunk.*

Anyway, I've resolved to be a little better about writing in my journal. And I've resolved to do better work back in Cubulco.

Graham had taken off midweek from Cubulco, a small town fifty kilometers north of Guatemala's capital. He hadn't been doing much. The people at the agency he was working with were having problems finding the 250 seedlings he needed for a project. He'd planned a huge *dia de campo* with the students and teachers of the local elementary school, complete with a piñata. They were going to spend the morning transplanting the seedlings on a mountain outside of town, then eat lunch, then play games. But he'd had to postpone the event twice, and he doubted it would ever happen. Frustrated and bored, he decided to leave Cubulco to travel around Guatemala, see places he'd always wanted to see. He had heard good things about Livingston. About the food. The culture. (The *indigenas* in Livingston, the Garifuna, were descendants not of the Maya but of Africans and were said to practice witchcraft.) So he left.

This is different from riding a bus. It's just as crowded, but it seems more dangerous somehow. There must be thirty of us here on top, maybe twice as many below. It must be market day in Puerto Barrios.

The water is rough. It's bad weather. It looks like it might rain soon. I can feel the boat rock.

People in Guatemala don't know how close they are to death sometimes. The bad busses. The rickety airplanes. This rotting ferry, wobbling on the waves.

Graham isn't hungry, although he's been waiting for Kathy, the nurse, for a long time. He calculates: The ferry left Livingston at five in the morning. It capsized probably an hour later, and it must have taken him forty-five minutes to swim to land, some anonymous ground, dense with trees, between Livingston and Puerto Barrios.

Sometime later, he saw a fisherman, trolling the waters about a hundred meters from shore. He waved frantically, and the fisherman rowed to where Graham was jumping and yelling and shaking a fistful of wet bills.

When Graham and the fisherman pulled out of the cove onto the rougher waters of the sea, Graham saw a single sleek body, black and lit from sunlight, rise from the waves and be helped over the edge into the safe dryness of a motor boat.

The rest of them? Graham wondered. The other people who were with him on the ferry? Where had they gone?

"There was an accident," Graham told the fisherman.

The fisherman nodded.

"The ferry sank."

The fisherman nodded again, his expression hidden beneath the shadow of his baseball cap.

La Prensa Libre, January 16. "Ferry Sinks Near Puerto Barrios."

A ferry carrying more than a hundred passengers from Livingston to Puerto Barrios in the *departamento* of Izabal capsized in the early hours yesterday morning, our regional correspondent reports.

The ferry, owned by Rapido Del Mar, left Livingston at five a.m. and capsized forty-five minutes into its journey. The only known survivor of the disaster was the ferry's captain, Ronaldo Ramirez of Bananera, Izabal. He was rescued by Sergio Morales, the owner of a private motorboat in Puerto Barrios. Morales, on his way to visit relatives in Livingston, noticed Ramirez clinging to a life preserver two kilometers from the coastline.

Admiral José Buenafe, head of the naval base in Puerto Barrios, ordered a special rescue team, which already has discovered an undisclosed number of bodies.

Disasters of this kind are not uncommon on the old, overcrowded ferries which twice daily make round-trip journeys from Livingston to Puerto Barrios. Last July, a ferry also capsized, although in shallow water, causing only minor injuries. Three years ago, however, thirty-eight people died when a ferry turned over three kilometers from the dock in Puerto Barrios.

Any minute Graham expects to see Kathy drive up in one of the Peace Corps' white Jeep Cherokees. Washed daily in the Peace Corps parking lot in the capital by a stooped and precise man named Manuel, they're always clean. Graham decides there won't be any dirt on Kathy's Cherokee even after the five-hour drive from the capital, although it includes a half-kilometer stretch of road where the highway's new asphalt was washed away in a flood. No, Graham thinks, Kathy and whoever comes with her will come as pure and swift as angels from the sky.

But he doesn't keep his eyes only on the road beside the hotel. He also looks at the sea, the rough Caribbean where the crests of waves glitter in the noon sunlight. He keeps expecting someone to be there. He keeps expecting to see them holding themselves above the waves.

I'll save them now, he thinks. I'll swim out and pull them to shore.

But even before he can envision the details of heroism, the particulars of salvation, he bows his head, knowing he wouldn't have the energy. He'd probably swum a mile in his shirt and shorts, his wallet still in his pocket. Yet when he reached shore, barefoot and exhausted, he swore he could still hear their voices. *Help me. I'm here.*

The only life he'd saved had been his own.

He feels the hotel shake, and he jumps to his feet. An earthquake. He runs to the top of the stairs. The stairs shake, and he's afraid he'll fall down them on his way to the lobby.

But maybe it isn't an earthquake, he thinks. Maybe the sea is rushing in—a tidal wave—and the hotel is adrift in water. He races to the porch, sees at first only water and thinks he and everyone in the hotel are in the middle of it. But can they swim? he wonders. If the hotel floods, can anyone in the hotel swim?

Can he swim now in his exhaustion? Is it his turn to drown?

With the hotel swaying like a bus rounding a curve, he turns from the rollicking sea and races toward the stairs. He grips the rail and stops.

I'm in a hotel, he thinks. I'm on land. There is no earthquake, no flood. I'm all right. All I need to do is wait.

Slowly, he turns from the stairs, walks back to the porch and sits in his chair with its view of both the road and the sea.

La Prensa Libre, January 17. "Mayor Says Citizens Should Learn to Swim"

Francisco Juarez, the mayor of Puerto Barrios, recommended yesterday that people traveling to and from his city by boat learn to swim in order to avoid the kind of tragedy that occurred two days ago when a passenger ferry from Livingston capsized.

Thirty-six bodies have been recovered from the water, and a search organized by Admiral José Buenafe, chief of the naval base in Puerto Barrios, is continuing.

Only two people are known to have survived the tragedy, Ronaldo Ramirez of Bananera, Izabal, and Graham Jourgan of the United States of America. Jourgan, working in Guatemala as a Peace Corps volunteer, was able to swim from the sinking ferry. He is being treated for exhaustion and stress at Cruz Roja Hospital in the capital.

The mayor said there are many shallow areas of the Caribbean Sea in and around Puerto Barrios, and he suggested citizens use them for swimming lessons. "We have so much water around us," he said, "and we are afraid of it."

Mayor Juarez admitted he is not able to swim, but said he plans to learn "as soon as possible."

"Do you want to talk about it, Graham?"

"Haven't I been talking about it?"

"Yes, of course. But you've only mentioned what happened before and after the ferry capsized. You've never talked about the moment it actually turned over. I think you might find it helpful."

"I don't remember. I remember writing in my journal. Or maybe I'd just put my journal away. Yeah, I'd just put it in my backpack. The boat was really rocking, and even though I was in front of the ferry and could see everything and had a nice breeze in my face, I was feeling sick."

"And then?"

"I don't remember."

At night, he tries to comfort himself by thinking of the boy he'd saved at camp. Graham was eighteen, a lifeguard, and Patrick, who at eight years old was the youngest boy in his cabin, was swimming in the deep end of the pool below the lifeguard's chair. Patrick had always hovered around Graham, and the other boys noticed this and called Patrick a baby.

Dog-paddling in the deep end, Patrick complained of a stomach cramp. Graham asked him if he could swim to the side of the pool. "No," Patrick said, but Graham didn't believe him. He thought Patrick only wanted attention.

"Are you sure?" Graham asked.

"Yes, I'm sure. Help. Help me."

Briefly, Graham thought of descending from his stand and using one of the poles on the side of the pool to rescue Patrick. But it was just as easy to jump in.

In the water, Graham lifted Patrick from under his shoulders and hauled him to the edge of the pool. "There," Graham said, and the dozen campers and two counselors who'd seen the rescue responded with mocking applause.

Graham had forgotten the incident until recently, but now he held on to the memory. I saved him, he told himself. I saved him. I saved him. I saved him.

This, like a mantra, until he could sleep.

November 11. Dear Uncle Eddie: Greetings from Cubulco, where I've lived now for five months. It's unbelievable how quickly the time has gone . . . .

Living here makes me think of all the advantages I've had because I'm an American, or North American, I should say. I play basketball on a team in town, and as you know from those peewee games you had to endure, I'm not a great player by any means, but here I'm a star. It's not only because I'm taller than most of the other players, it's also because I have more skills. Why? Because when I was growing up, I had the time to learn how to play. When they're not in school, most boys here are helping their parents in the fields.

There are so many little things I know how to do because I had the time, things like juggling (I've impressed a lot of people by juggling three balls—imagine what kind of reaction the Flying Karamazov Brothers would get), doing a cartwheel and swimming. It's amazing how many people in town don't know how to swim. I know this because when I got here, I practiced my Spanish by asking everyone "*Puede usted nadar?*" Can you swim?

"You couldn't have saved any of them. You were lucky, very lucky, to have saved yourself."

"I still feel guilty."

"Why?"

"Because I could swim. And they couldn't."

"You have a skill, a skill that isn't common in Guatemala. You used it to save yourself. The captain of the ferry had a life preserver. He used it to save himself. Everybody on that boat would have used whatever they could have to save themselves."

"But don't you think it's unfair? I mean, in addition to being a rich American, I know how to swim. It would have been fairer if who lived and who died had come down to who could make the best tortilla. Then those people would at least have had a chance."

"If it had come down to who could make the best tortilla, you would have died."

"Maybe that would have been fairer."

"Traveling?"

The man is blond-haired with a slight sunburn. He carries in his arms a blond baby, also with a slight sunburn.

Graham looks up at him from his chair on the second-floor porch of Hotel Del Norte. "No, I'm not traveling. Or, well, yes." Can he tell the man what happened? The man isn't from the States. His accent sounds German.

"Where have you been?" the man asks.

"To Livingston."

"Yes, Livingston. I am going to Livingston tomorrow with my son." The man looks down at the blond baby in his arms. "We are traveling by the ferry."

"Do you know how to swim?"

"Yes."

"Does your son?"

The man chuckles. "No, he's only a baby. But perhaps he would float. You know, the baby fat."

"I could have saved a baby. I mean, a baby isn't hard to carry."

"A mile?"

"I'm a good swimmer. I could have swum with a baby in one hand."

"In rough waters for one mile?"

"I could have. Easily."

"Even to get to a baby, you would have . . . well, you would have exposed yourself to the others. They all would have tried to grab you. Do you think you could have reached a baby before they grabbed you and pulled you under? You were faced with an impossible situation. You did the only thing you could have done."

La Prensa Libre, February 1. "Mayor Takes a Swimming Lesson."

Puerto Barrios Mayor Francisco Juarez took a swimming lesson yesterday at the Aguas Azules Recreation Plaza in an effort to promote public safety. The mayor said he hopes others follow his example in order to avoid the kind of tragedy that befell passengers of a ferry traveling from Livingston to Puerto Barrios last month. Sixty-eight people died in the tragedy, and seven people believed to have been on the ferry have not been found.

"There is no shame in learning something new," said the 55-year-old mayor, who received his swimming lesson from Mario De La Cruz Polanco, a local physical education instructor. "The shame is in not trying to learn."

Graham had learned to swim in first grade when his teacher, Ms. Robinson, took the class twice weekly to the swimming pool at Chester Arthur Senior High School. He remembered an array of learning tools: red kickboards with pictures of dolphins, Styrofoam tubes shaped like giant Tootsie Rolls, inflated yellow ducks with encouraging messages—*Keep kicking!*—written on their necks. Most of all he remembered Ms. Robinson, a large black woman who always wore a T-shirt over her bathing suit.

He remembered her holding him up by the stomach, and how soft her hands were and how sometimes they fluttered under him like wings. Even in the water, he was ticklish. When he laughed, he swallowed water, and Ms. Robinson would help him to the edge and pat him lightly on the back.

"How long were you in Guatemala?"

"A little over a year."

"You think you'll go back?"

"I'm on, you know, medical leave. I have another two weeks to decide. Really, I don't know. I mean . . . I don't know."

"It must be tough, man."

"It is."

"Your shot."

"Oh. Right."

What he might have told Paul but couldn't in the thick smoke of the bar, their beers on the edge of the pool table, was that even if he never went back to Guatemala, he feared he'd always be there.

It was harder to sleep now. He'd lost Patrick. When he closed his eyes, the scene from camp merged with the waters of the Caribbean. Patrick's was the lone white face in a crowd of brown and black faces, all of them holding steady above the rocking water. *I am here. Help me.* He couldn't save Patrick now. He could only save himself.

I saved myself. So what, damn it. I saved myself. I saved myself. I'm alive. I'm alive. I'm alive.

I saved myself. I'm sorry. I'm alive, and I'm sorry.

"What'd you say?"

Graham looked up at Paul, whose lips held a cigarette. He had an impulse to grab the cigarette and hurl it into the corner. He didn't understand why people wanted to kill themselves.

"I said it's your shot."

On the porch of Hotel Del Norte, Graham thinks of the other people who have come here. He pictures sea captains, drinking rum and laughing over bad jokes. He imagines banana company executives smoking cigars and dreaming of dark-haired women in the red-curtained bars a few blocks away. He imagines a lonely ship's clerk, pacing the uneven floor, worried about his sick mother back in New York.

The place already has ghosts, he thinks, trying to comfort himself. The place is already haunted. Even if the ferry had never sunk, there still would be voices here. Ghosts. He tries to hear their voices, the voices of people who'd been guests of the hotel years before, but all he hears are voices from the sea.

Help me. I'm here.

Where are you, Kathy? He stands and begins to pace. Where are you?

He'd asked the woman at the hotel desk to send his telegram *urgente*. It should have arrived at the Peace Corps office hours ago.

La Extra, January 20. "Captain Speaks About the Day His Ferry Sank."

My name is Ronaldo Ramirez, and I was the captain of the ferry that sank five days ago coming from Livingston.

The boat was very crowded, with many people on the lower deck and the top. It was a market day in Puerto Barrios, so people from Livingston were bringing their goods to sell. We'd had to leave many people behind. Even so, we had too many on board. The owners of the ferry demand a full cargo. I no longer work for these men.

The water was not particularly rough, but rough enough. I think there must have been a big ship nearby, it was not easy to tell in the early light, but the waves grew more violent, and then a big wave hit hard enough to knock us over.

I remember very well falling into the water, and I remember thinking that I would die. Yes, I do know how to swim, but I felt many hands grabbing me and pulling me under. I was ready to die. I had given myself over to the will of God. I swallowed a lot of water.

But then I was able to breathe. I was all alone and holding a life preserver. I do not know how this life preserver came to be in my hands. I consider it a miracle, an act of God. People have said that I was cruel to use the life preserver when I could swim, but I say honestly that the life preserver was put into my hands by God.

March 15. Dear Susan:

I hope this letter finds you despite all those books you're buried under. Your first year is almost history. Congratulations!

Thanks for asking about Graham. He's doing much better than when you saw him.

When he first came home, he tried to talk about what happened. That's what the psychologist suggested he do, but he didn't say much. Then one night he came into my room. It was late, and he'd just woken up from a nap. He'd been sleeping a lot, even though he'd been having bad dreams. He asked if I had time to talk, and of course I said yes.

He said he remembered one couple. The woman was very heavy, with thick thighs and a large, round face. She was wearing a short red dress and earrings. The man wasn't skinny, but he wasn't nearly as heavy as the woman and he was tall, about Graham's height. He was a good-looking guy, very dark-skinned with a clean-cut Afro. The man was standing beside the woman at the railing and they were both laughing like they were at the circus. Graham said he found it so heartening that they were able to share this laughter. He said he thought of Mom and Dad, and wondered if they'd ever been so happy together. Then the ferry began to shake and the woman started to tremble and the man spoke to her, to comfort her, but then Graham couldn't hear him anymore because everyone began to scream.

Graham said to me, "Maybe it will be easier if I get to know them all. Maybe I can mourn them if I remember each one."

He tried to tell me about some others on the boat, but he didn't remember anyone else, not really. He said he thought he remembered some faces, but he couldn't say whether he'd seen them on the ferry or somewhere else.

Graham is back in Guatemala now, and Mom got a letter from him two days ago. He seems to be doing all right. Of course, he still thinks about what happened, but he feels an obligation to finish his service. He has only a year left. And like he said, he can't possibly feel any worse about the situation, no matter where he is.

March 20. Sorry. I forgot to put this in the mail. In the meantime I got a letter from Graham, who seems to be doing *much* better. He told me I should dump Peter if Peter keeps seeing Linda. It's nice having an older brother looking out for me even if he's a thousand miles away.

La Prensa Libre, January 16. "Ceremony Marks Anniversary of Drownings."

More than three hundred people came to the seashore at Puerto Barrios today to remember the seventy-five passengers who drowned on this date last year when a ferry from Livingston to Puerto Barrios capsized.

The mourners spent the early morning at a memorial service led by Father Guillermo Santiago in the Santa María Catholic Church, then walked to the sea, where they dropped flowers in the water.

Later, the group gathered in the central park for a speech by Puerto Barrios Mayor Francisco Juarez. Mayor Juarez told the somber gathering that he was sure such a tragedy would never occur again.

"I have encouraged the teaching of swimming in all of our schools," the mayor said. "Before the tragedy, I myself couldn't swim. Now I swim every weekend with my family."

Whenever he traveled—on a bus, a train, a plane—Graham thought of the ferry. He wondered how long he would have this association. Forever, he thought, although not, as before, with panic. He would remember for the rest of his life, and this was all right. It was the least he could do for the seventy-five people who'd died. His memory would be a small memorial

Even when he wasn't traveling, he remembered. Something as common as water dripping from the tap could set him thinking about the people who had drowned. He knew without a doubt that he couldn't have saved any of them, although sometimes he fantasized about what it would have been like to have saved them all, pulling them in a long string to shore. And sometimes still, at too late an hour, he believed he at least could have rescued a baby.

But more often, his dreams were gentle, and sometimes even in waking hours the dead comforted him, appearing before him on the top of waves like angels, wings beating like the wings of hummingbirds, a quick dance above the water before they flew up to be embraced by the blue sky. Sometimes he saw their faces, and he didn't think it mattered that they were probably not their real faces, it only mattered that they looked at him and that sometimes, most times, he didn't turn away but waited for them to rise to the sky.

In his last week in Guatemala, Graham and the children from the Cubulco Elementary School planted 250 seedlings, securing them to their new soil by molding dirt around their pencil-thin trunks. Afterwards, they broke open a piñata and ate a lunch prepared by the school's teachers, who, afterwards, urged Graham to make a speech. He thought of telling them that the trees were for the seventy-five people who had drowned on the ferry from Livingston, but he wasn't thinking this as he'd planted the trees and he decided it would be false to say so now. The trees, he figured, were for the trees themselves, each life lived in the presence of other lives but ultimately alone.

Leaving the mountain, carrying the six-year-old son of one of the teachers on his shoulders, Graham sensed it was about to rain. He knew he could think that it was ironic, how in some situations water could be deadly but in others its absence became equally fatal. Instead he was comfortable knowing that things held their opposite, water being both fierce and sustaining. Life had in it always the possibility of death.

A few minutes later, it did begin to rain, but no one screamed in panic, no one flailed. This water was welcome, and Graham welcomed it by opening his mouth.

El Pastor, March. "La Iglesia de Dios Welcomes New Minister."

Ronaldo Ramirez, who completed seminary training in Guatemala City last month, will serve as pastor of our church in Dolores, Petén. With his wife, Cruz, and three children, Señor Morales will move to the remote pueblo this week and begin holding services in April.

Before going to the seminary, Señor Ramirez was a sea captain. He said he decided to become a minister when a ferry he was piloting from Livingston to Puerto Barrios capsized in rough waters three years ago and he was one of only two people on board to survive the tragedy.

"I felt the hand of God," Señor Ramirez said. "I want others to know His healing grace."

Graham hears Kathy's Jeep Cherokee before he sees it, and he stands and walks to the side of the second-story porch. Thank God, he thinks. He wants, suddenly, to cry.

In seconds, the car appears at the end of the dusty road, then pulls into the parking lot. Graham leaves the porch, races down the stairs and steps out the front door.

"Hey there," Kathy says, closing the Cherokee's door.

Graham has imagined their conversation many times, but he's nervous now, afraid he won't be able to speak.

She says something, but he doesn't hear her, only thinks he hears her, and he responds quickly, defensively: "I couldn't face calling, Kathy. I couldn't do it. I . . . ." He feels something catch in his throat.

"I didn't say you should have called," Kathy says gently. "You did fine to send the telegram. Now, tell me, what's wrong?"

"I . . . ." He stops on his words and sees, behind Kathy, someone coming from the Jeep. Kathy is dressed in blue jeans and a red blouse, but her companion, the large black woman, wears a clean white nurse's uniform.

"Who came with you?" he asks, pointing behind her.

Kathy turns, stares a few seconds, then turns around again. "I came alone, Graham."

Graham looks at Kathy, who is frowning with concern. There are crow's feet around her hazel eyes and streaks of gray in her short, brown hair. She is older than he remembered, even though he saw her only a month or two before. Perhaps she's forty, perhaps she's as old as his mother. Her age comforts him, as if it alone is capable of forgiving him.

He looks again behind her, but there is no one there.

"She's gone," Graham says.

"Who's gone?"

"They're all gone."

He feels foolish crying in Kathy's arms when she doesn't even know yet what happened.

English Spoken But Not Understood.

Whenever Martha comes to Café Americano, she sits in front of these words, painted in red letters with blue stripes on a white canvas. A decade ago, one of her predecessors commissioned the sign from a street corner artist and presented it to Sergio, the café's owner, who proved a good sport by hanging it above the grill. Sergio probably hadn't intended to keep the sign on display forever, but it quickly became as much a part of the café's reputation as its chicken *caldo* and stove-fried tortillas.

Here again to report on a political crisis, Martha waits less than ten minutes to see the sign's motto fulfilled. When an older American couple—he in his sixties, she perhaps a decade younger—ask Hidalia, the new waitress with a healthy growth of hair above her lip, if sitting so close to the window is safe, she says, "Okay, I clean it for you." And belying the café's reputation for slow and inhospitable service, Hidalia returns a moment later with a damp rag.

The couple now have a clear view of whatever uprising might occur on the street. The man casts his eyes down, as if in prayer, as his wife, with a worried purse of her lips, shakes her head. Sitting at the counter with her hamburger and *papas fritas*, Martha catches the woman's eye. "You've got the best seats in the house," she tells her.

The woman tries to smile. "We came to see the ruins, the temples. But at the airport this morning we were told we couldn't leave the capital because of the . . . the . . . ." She turns to her husband. "What's it called?"

"Self-coup," he says. "We knew the country was unstable, but we didn't expect this."

"It's the country's first *autogolpe*," Martha says. "I've covered three traditional coups here."

"You're a reporter?" the man asks.

Martha nods.

"Television?"

"Print." She tells them the name of her magazine, adding, "the international version."

"Ah," they say appreciatively.

The radio sitting on a shelf behind the counter is playing marimba music, a telltale sign of a coup. No station would dare broadcast reports of what is happening lest it offend whoever is in power—or whoever will assume power next. The childlike sound gives Café Americano the air of a birthday party.

It is a quarter past nine. Outside, an occasional car rushes past on the street. Otherwise, the street is deserted.

At noon, Martha stood with other reporters in a windowless room in the basement of the Presidential Palace. The president's chief of staff, a short, bald man in a blue pinstriped suit, said the president had seized power because in attempting to prosecute him for his supposed embezzlement of public funds, the congress was covering up its own corruption. "This is a coup," said the chief of staff, speaking English for the benefit of the foreign reporters, "for the good of the country. You may label it a self-coup. But we call it a selfless coup." Martha was sure the chief of staff had invented the phrase because after he spoke it, he grinned with an author's pride.

Somewhere in the night the country's military leaders are meeting to determine whether they will back the president or depose him. Martha doesn't know where they are meeting. Even if she did, she wouldn't bother to stake out a place in front of it. The men who know the truth are usually reticent to talk; the uninformed are all too eager to spill self-promotional blather.

Thanks to Sergio, Martha doesn't need to go anywhere. Sergio seems to have connections in all branches of the military—indeed, in all of the country's places of power—and during coups and other political crises, he is Martha's chief informant. She didn't always trust him. But when six and a half years ago during the first coup she covered events that unfolded as he foretold, with three generals forming a junta and quelling street riots and protests at the national university, she concluded he was more than he seemed. In the coup's aftermath, with the streets stripped even of beggars and dogs, she spent five nights with him. Holed up in his two-bedroom apartment, they lived off stale tortillas and bottles of Chilean wine with twist-off tops.

During subsequent occasions of unrest, not every piece of Sergio's information proved correct, but most of it did, and what he told her inevitably contained more truth than what her other contacts revealed. Whenever she asks about his sources, he replies, in English, "Friends." He insists on speaking English with her, although she is fluent in Spanish. Even when they make love, he speaks English. If at first she found it disconcerting to be the recipient of a repertoire of endearments culled from American pop songs, she now finds it endearing and faintly forbidden, as if she were bedding down with a teenager.

Martha has long suspected that Sergio is from one of the country's Four Families. He has never admitted as much, but when Martha prods him, he always gives her a mischievous smile and a slow, knowing wink. Besides, Sergio looks like an aristocrat: he's slim, with an angular build and a delicate mustache.

"You must lead an exciting life," says the woman at the table near the window.

"I've seen a lot of Latin American history up close," Martha admits. "I've covered three wars, four assassinations, six coups, and one regional peace conference."

She'd wanted to be a foreign correspondent ever since she was twelve years old and her parents bought her a video camera. She made an anchor's desk out of a coffee table and hung a world map behind it, and she played the well-traveled reporter, using a yardstick to point to countries enduring revolutions and famines and floods. Later, she added romance to her fantasy—liaisons with strong-jawed generals and long-haired, poetry-spouting revolutionaries. The job, as she imagined it, was thrilling.

After graduating from Smith, Martha spent two years writing news copy at PNBC in Philadelphia. She made a pair of on-camera appearances, but her dark, thick eyebrows, longish nose and full mouth appeared, in the distorting prism of the camera, cartoonish. Knowing her path to becoming a foreign correspondent would be impeded if she insisted on a television career, she moved to print journalism.

"When is your deadline?" the man asks.

"In two hours."

"You seem so casual about it."

"I have most of what I need." Martha taps her reporter's notebook at the side of her plate of French fries, although she is thinking of Sergio, wondering what news he is uncovering over the telephone in his office at the back of the café.

Sergio is the only man she makes love to anymore. Two years ago, she dated Antonio, a deputy to Italy's ambassador in Buenos Aires, where she is based. Three months into their relationship, she found, under towels in a closet, a photograph of him posing with a woman and three children in the central square of an Italian hamlet. When she confronted him, he spoke with half a smile and without shame: "Ah, you have discovered my family."

When a man who has been sitting at the back of the café slips out the door and onto the quiet street, the woman by the window turns to Martha again. "It *is* safe to leave, isn't it?"

"You didn't hear any gunshots, did you?" Martha says. When the woman doesn't smile, Martha adds, "I'm joking."

"Well, good," the woman says uncertainly, picking up the second half of her sandwich before thinking better of it and returning it to her plate. "I told Jim we should eat at the hotel restaurant, but he took one look at the prices and said they must be charging extra because of the coup."

"The hotel's only a block away," her husband says, shrugging. "And we're both former cross-country runners." He forces a laugh before turning to look out the window.

Four months ago, Martha flew in from Buenos Aires to write a freelance travel piece. She'd mapped an ambitious itinerary, which included white-water rafting and spelunking in the northern mountains. But instead of riding the rapids of the Río Profundo or inching past bats in the Moreno Caves, she ended up spending all six days in the capital with Sergio, going with him to museums and movies in the afternoon and, at night, curling up with him under his wool blanket.

On their penultimate night together, Sergio took her dancing at Disco Tropical, a club on the border of good and bad neighborhoods and patronized by a mixture of classes and races, rare to see in the country. They'd danced, had glasses of rum mixed with mango juice, danced again. A group of Americans came into the club, and Sergio introduced her to them—they were teaching English at the capital's most exclusive private high school. With her permission, he danced with one of the women. Seeing them move in an effortless salsa, Martha grew suspicious; their ease suggested familiarity in other places.

Later, in bed, she was cool to him, and after failing to break her mood with queries about what was bothering her, he crooned a line from a country-western song popular at the time: "You are my one, darlin', my sun, my moon, my blue lagoon." He pronounced the last word *Le Goon*, and, envisioning a French henchman with a blue vein zigzagging down his forehead, she laughed. Usually, this would have been enough to dispatch whatever troubled her, but she found it difficult to shake the image of Sergio dancing with the American woman.

As she gazed at Sergio in the partial darkness, she imagined them in another, larger room, in a larger house. It was a nice thought: the Latin American blue blood and the American correspondent, at home. She listened to his breathing—it was light and without snores, as if he'd somehow been bred to have good manners even in sleep—and she found herself wishing she could live the same scene more than only a few nights a year. Even when she woke the next morning to find the room cold and cramped, she was reluctant to leave.

The older couple call Hidalia for the check. "Next year, we're going to the Bahamas," the woman says, standing and brushing crumbs from her blouse.

Martha wishes them luck. "We'll look for your story," the man says. She watches them hurry down the block to the Hotel Dorado like people caught in the rain without an umbrella.

She is the only patron left in the café. Hidalia comes to pick up the dishes left by the departing couple. After hauling them to the kitchen, she sits three stools down from Martha and stares at her with what, thanks to her mustache, seems like sinister curiosity. "You're waiting for Sergio," Hidalia says in Spanish.

"Yes, I am."

"Why?"

"To talk."

"You're writing a story." Hidalia nods toward Martha's notebook. "You are the *periodista*."

"I guess I am." Martha keeps her voice friendly, although Hidalia seems to have embarked on an inquisition. "What have you heard about me?"

"Sergio says one thing to his friends. He says another to my sister."

"Who is your sister?"

She ignores the question. Gesturing with her chin toward Sergio's office, Hidalia says, "He is only a café owner."

"I know he's a café owner."

Hidalia laughs. "But you think he knows important people."

Martha doesn't reply—she pretends to review her notes. When, half a minute later, she looks up, Hidalia is still staring at her. "You don't know him," Hidalia says.

Martha gives her a condescending smile. "Do you?"

"I know the truth."

"What is the truth?"

"Ask him yourself," Hidalia says.

A minute after Hidalia's challenge, Sergio steps out of his office. He is wearing black slacks, a tan sport coat and a red button-down shirt with no tie. He gives Martha a large smile and motions her to the table abandoned by the older American couple. Martha takes a quick look at Hidalia before sitting across from Sergio.

"This will happen . . . ." Sergio begins, speaking softly to keep Hidalia, who remains sitting on her counter stool, from hearing. "This will happen," he repeats in an even quieter voice. He brings his hands from under the table and places them in front of him. They are unusually large hands, with thin, graceful fingers. "Tomorrow or the next day or the day following, the president will lose support from the military. He will go to Panama or Paraguay."

"Why doesn't he have the military's support?" Martha asks.

Sergio considers this. "The military cannot help a dictator anymore. This is, how do you say, new age." He pauses, corrects himself: "*A* new age. The military looks bad now. Bad reputation. They don't want to look . . . how do you say . . . more bad by helping a dictator. The military must do what looks right."

"The military will support the vice president?"

"The military will follow the law. When president is gone, vice president is president."

From her seat on the counter stool, Hidalia laughs. Because of the way the café's fluorescent lights strike her, her mustache glistens. "She thinks you've been talking to generals and colonels," she announces in Spanish. "She thinks you know important people."

"I know important people," Sergio says. In a firmer voice, he tells Hidalia, "It's time to go home. I will close the café tonight."

Hidalia leaves her seat and takes a few steps toward them, her arms swinging to her sides as if she is preparing to draw pistols. "Do you know who he was talking to?" she says. "He was talking to Francisco, who is a barber, and Mario, who owns a cantina, and Oswaldo, who is a ticket-taker at Cine Capital." Hidalia crosses her arms over her chest and locks her eyes on Sergio. "Tell her the truth and see if she feels about you the way Gisela does." She pivots and retreats to the kitchen, the wooden door flapping in her wake.

"What's her problem?" Martha asks.

"Problem?" Sergio replies.

"Why would she lie about you?"

There is a pause, and Martha wonders if he has understood her. Sergio's eyes are still trained on the kitchen door, as if he is expecting Hidalia to return with another onslaught. He sighs. "She wants Gisela, her sister . . . "

"But she *is* lying," Martha interrupts. It's half an affirmation, half a question.

"Lying . . . well . . . "

"Wait," Martha says. "Is she lying or isn't she?"

Sergio seems taken aback by Martha's question, as if he didn't expect resistance from her side.

"You haven't been talking with anyone in power?" she asks.

"Power?"

"*Poder*," she says, hoping to gain some clarity by switching to Spanish. He winces as if she'd insulted him.

In English, he says, "Power. I understand power. But the men with the power . . . they have it like air in their hands. Four times you come to write about changes in power, and where are the men now? Gone . . . or dead."

"Who have you been talking to, Sergio?"

"If I tell you, you will go to them." He looks her over a little mournfully before smiling. It's the smile he uses to stop her from prying about his sources or former lovers.

"Do you know the generals?"

"I know," he says, "what I know."

"You never talk to the generals—to anyone in power?"

"I tell you what will happen. I talk to people who know."

"You knew what I believed about you, Sergio. You knew I thought you had family connections in important places."

His smile fades. "I give you what you need."

"You were talking to a barber?"

"Okay," he says. "I will tell you this much, his name: Francisco Juarez. He is called *El Barbero*. He knows everyone."

"Sergio," she says, amazed at how quickly her certainty about who he was has fled, replaced by a queasy, hung-over feeling, "I could ask anyone to *guess* what will happen in this country. I could go around the corner and ask the shoeshine boys in the park."

"I give you what you need," he repeats.

She feels oddly exposed in the dim lights of the café, the potential object of ridicule, as if her editor were watching from a hidden camera. "I thought you were from one of the Four Families."

"Poor family." He nods slowly, as if ashamed. "Okay, I will tell you now. Now is time to tell. I come from a poor family."

"Four Families." She holds up four fingers. "I thought you were from one of the Four Families."

"Ah," he says, waving, "most of them are dead."

"But they are powerful."

"Dead." He makes a low, cooing sound, an imitation of a ghost.

Staring at his bony shoulders and his scant, ungraceful mustache, she wonders how she could ever have mistaken him for the wayward son of one of the country's dynasties.

He reaches toward her, putting his hands on her shoulders. "Tonight," he says, "I want to speak in a sincere way. I am no . . . how do you say . . . spring of the chicken."

"Spring chicken," she says, correcting him mechanically, her thoughts elsewhere. She wonders where she veered into her fantasy of him. Was it on their first night together, when he touched her hair, lifting it lovingly behind her ears? "'Spring chicken' is the phrase."

"Yes, correct," he says. "I am at the hour when I must think about my future. I am at two roads crossing. Crossing roads. I . . . yes . . . I would like, at last, to marry. I have interest in one girl. Gisela, sister of Hidalia. Nice girl. Nicer than Hidalia. But you I am in love with." He gives her an uncertain smile. When she fails to meet it with an encouraging response, it falls quickly into a frown.

All this time, she thinks, *I have been relying on the political insights of a barber. And all this time I have been sleeping with a . . . with a . . . .* "Sergio, Sergio," she says, feeling at least certain of his name, "I can't possibly talk about this now. I believed—and you encouraged me to believe—you were someone else."

"But what I give to you . . . "

She interrupts: "You'll have to tell me who this barber is and who he talks to. Does he cut the generals' hair? And these other men, how do they know what's going to happen? Who do they know? Or have their guesses been lucky?"

"In time, I will tell you," he says. "But first, I would like to hear what you think of what I said to you."

"I don't have much time, Sergio. My deadline, remember? Will you please answer my questions?" She knows her tone is wrong. It would be wrong with a man who wasn't her lover. It is especially wrong now. But she feels annoyed by her gullibility and the carefree way he allowed her to keep her illusion. He must have relished telling his friends how his American girlfriend believed he was the reluctant heir to a fortune.

"Come on, Sergio. I need to know who these men are and who they know."

A deep crease forms in his forehead. His mustache appears to be trembling. She looks around and notices the ripped orange plastic cascading off of one of the counter stools and the spiderweb cracks in the yellow wallpaper above the booths.

"Will you tell me?"

Sergio turns away from her, staring into the street.

She pushes her chair back with a loud scraping sound and stands up. "I have a story to write," she says. "We'll talk later, all right?"

She waits for him to turn back to her. He doesn't.

"I have a story to write," she repeats, this time more like an apology. She picks up her notebook and walks to the door. She pauses, thinking he'll say something, call her back. When she hears nothing, she pushes open the door and steps into the night.

As if to punish Sergio, Martha ignores his information, and her story's lead quotes the president's chief of staff calling the coup "selfless." The story ends, "But it will be up to the military to decide whether the president's self-coup is in the best interest of the country. And, so far, military leaders are keeping their intentions to themselves."

She has gone past her deadline by fifteen minutes, and her editor isn't in a good mood. "I could have gotten this off the wire," he says over the telephone from Mexico City. "What are your sources in the military saying?"

"They aren't."

"They're letting you down," he says. "The bastards."

She hears him punching his computer keys. "Okay, we'll go with it. Stay in country and keep following the story."

She waits by the phone in her room at the Hotel Dorado to see if her editor has any questions for her. She flips on the television, but all the local channels seem to be showing Mexican movies from the 1960s. As she watches a clown dance around a bullring, she remembers going to the circus with Sergio. It had been his idea, and, with wild promises of what was inside, he'd encouraged her into the single tent perched on an abandoned lot. After the first act, which consisted of two monkeys playing off-key duets on a piano and a clown strumming mournfully on a guitar, she made a show of yawning and fidgeting—she had, she remembers, only a day or two left in the country and she didn't want to waste it on a third-rate circus. Conceding to her boredom, he'd taken her back to his apartment.

Before they went to sleep, he asked her what she thought the rest of the circus had been like, what acts had followed the monkeys and the clown, and she replied, "More nonsense." Now she winces at her brevity. She'd aborted his opportunity to do what he'd probably never done as a child. She'd even denied him the lesser pleasure of imagining what had followed the one skit he had seen.

She stands up and walks to the door, thinking she'll go to Sergio's apartment. But on the street she might be stopped, questioned, detained. She walks to the large window at the end of the room. From it, she can see the outlines of a volcano, the country's second largest. Periodically, its peak flares with an orange splash of lava.

Martha wonders if Sergio will come to her hotel room, as he usually does late on nights of her deadline. She thinks about his hands around her waist and how she always thought of them as powerful hands, the hands of someone who might have been a general or a cabinet minister.

Whenever she asked about his family, he said, "I have chosen a different path," and she imagined this as a reasonable decision, Sergio choosing to live a simpler, less public (and, therefore, safer) life than he might have. One night, after they'd finished a bottle of wine, he described playing soccer as a boy. The field was near the ocean, and he described the salt-taste of the air and the wind's dampness. His recall had been so vivid she'd assumed the experience was singular, part of a memorable coastal vacation his family had taken. When she asked him this, he said, "I have given up playing soccer." Thinking he'd misunderstood her question, she let the subject drop. But if she took his soccer soliloquy as autobiography, she might conclude he grew up in one of the poor coastal towns, Costa Azul or Playa Gorda; he might be a sailor's son, a fisherman's son.

Her editor doesn't call, so she draws a bath. Sinking into it, she tries to relax.

From outside, she hears what sounds like a gunshot. She wonders if Sergio is the kind of man who would be devastated by their exchange tonight. She doubts it. Nevertheless, she follows the fantasy of his suicide.

She sees herself at his funeral, at the back of the church, murmuring, "I loved him," and, alternately, "I didn't know him."

She tries to feel what she would feel, but she doesn't feel anything save the bathwater growing cool around her.

Her alarm wakes her at seven. She shuts it off. This is followed by a wake-up call from the hotel. She says, "Gracias," hangs up and rolls over. Her next deadline isn't until the following week.

At nine o'clock, she rises, uses the bathroom, and brings her toothbrush into the main room to brush as she watches television. She sees a news clip of a well-dressed man walking up long stairs into the body of an airplane. She hears the announcer's voice-over: "At seven o'clock this morning, President Gonzalez departed the country for Paraguay."

She feels she has already seen this footage, as if she dreamed it.

She drops her toothbrush, gets dressed and hails a taxi to

the Presidential Palace. It is raining, and the taxi has difficulty navigating the crowded streets. Despite the bad weather, people have come out to celebrate.

Martha is one of three dozen reporters standing in the pressroom in the basement. "We didn't even eat breakfast," she hears a reporter from CNN tell a reporter from a Mexican station. "We were at the airport at seven, but we missed his plane by five minutes. Who got the shot of him?"

"We did," the Mexican says.

"How'd you hear he would be at the airport?"

The Mexican doesn't reply.

More than an hour passes before a spokesman for the vice president steps into the room. "The people have spoken," he says at the beginning of a long statement touting the country's commitment to democracy.

In his report outside the Presidential Palace, the CNN reporter says, "The new president may credit the people with having spoken, but it was the military who had the last word here."

Martha has left her umbrella in the taxi, but she doesn't mind the rain. It's swift but warm, and she accepts the soaking as part of her penance.

An hour later, the rain has stopped. Martha, in dry clothes, sits in the patio behind her hotel, flipping through her notebook. It is full of quotes and observations. By the time she writes about the aftermath of the self-coup, however, it will be old news. If she's lucky, her editor will give her a paragraph in the "World Briefs" section.

She thinks about going to the Café Americano, but decides against it, in part because Sergio's information was correct, as usual, and she is embarrassed by having questioned his sources. More than this, however, she is reluctant to see Sergio because her displeasure with his deception has waned, replaced by curiosity. But whether her curiosity is of a woman intrigued by a man she doesn't entirely know but loves or only of a reporter eager to follow a story to its conclusion, she isn't sure. The afternoon passes until, recollecting herself, she says aloud, "I am a foreign correspondent."

She repeats the phrase slowly, hoping the words will resonate in the rain-softened air like an affirmation. But there is no grand echo, and she is left to stare at what is in front of her: the empty swimming pool, the dozen roses growing crooked and gnarled in clay pots, the three pigeons huddled like mourners under a mango tree.

At the end of the day, she has dinner with Frank, the CNN reporter, at the hotel restaurant. Frank is a decade older than she and his hair has retreated to an inch or two short of his crown. On television, however, he looks distinguished and trustworthy. After three drinks, he asks her if she'd like to come up to his room.

"You're married," she tells him.

"Yes I am." As if to confirm it, he holds up his left hand and points to his wedding ring. "It's your only chance," he says. "We're leaving tomorrow."

"So soon?"

"The story is over." Smiling, he adds, "For the time being, anyway. Wait until the generals start hating the new president."

She rides the elevator with Frank to the fifth floor, where they both have rooms, and says goodnight to him in the hallway. He takes his rejection without bitterness. He even blows her a kiss.

In bed, trying to sleep, she hears the sounds of celebration on the street below. Firecrackers go off periodically. Even when Martha puts a pillow over her head, she hears their accelerating crackle and their loud, finishing bang.

Martha is one of the few foreign reporters who remain in country on the second day after President Gonzalez's exile. On the third day, she is the only foreign reporter. On the fourth day, she files her story. Her editor tells her he probably won't use it.

That night, in an effort to resist going to Café Americano, she finds herself in Cine Capital, watching a movie she never would have bothered to see in Buenos Aires. It is, in fact, a sequel to a movie she never would have seen. The sound quality is poor. She contents herself with eating stale popcorn, finding errors in the subtitles, and tearing up inexplicably during swells of the sentimental score.

After the movie, she goes to the hotel bar and orders a Jack Daniel's. At a table at the back of the bar, she sees the same older couple she saw in Café Americano. They must have completed their tour of the temples. Concerned they might spot her, Martha picks up her drink and walks to a table near the window. She spends an hour alternately watching people pass on the street and gazing at the reflection of her face.

She finishes three drinks and returns to her room. But she cannot sleep, even with no firecrackers exploding outside her window.

She remembers what Hidalia said about Sergio: "He's only a café owner." *Yes*, she thinks, *but he knows how to work his sources. He's a better reporter than I am.*

She thinks about whether she could marry Sergio, about how it might work. She could probably talk her editor into allowing her to live here. It's as accessible to the rest of Latin America as Buenos Aires. Or perhaps Sergio would move with her to Argentina. He would like her apartment. On her balcony, with its vivid view of the city, they could spend long evenings conjuring all kinds of circus acts. The image makes her laugh and, at the same time, encourages her, gives her hope and a faint rush of joy.

When Martha steps up to the door of Café Americano, it is a quarter to ten. Inside, she sees Hidalia mopping the floor. She tries the door, but it's locked, so she knocks. Hidalia looks up; it takes her a minute to stroll to the door and open it. "Sergio isn't here," she says.

"Where is he?"

When Hidalia doesn't respond, Martha asks again, with urgency.

With a triumphant curl of her upper lip, Hidalia says, "*They* are at his apartment."

If Martha had thought more seriously about it, she would have been suspicious of where Sergio lives. If it isn't a destitute neighborhood, it is a dozen blocks from the city's wealthiest districts, and even someone who had broken from his rich family would probably have chosen to live in a more respectable area. To Martha, however, Sergio's apartment, located on the second floor of an unpainted blockhouse, always seemed a clever part of his disguise.

Uncertain about what will happen, Martha tells the cab driver to wait. Looking around at the desolate street, he says, "All right, but hurry." She climbs the outside stairs to the second floor and taps on the door. She sees no light in any of the windows, but she figures Sergio couldn't have left the café long ago. When no one answers, she knocks louder.

She hears a woman's voice: "Quién es?"

Unnerved, Martha doesn't reply. When the woman asks again, Martha gives her name. The door opens, and she sees Hidalia standing in front of her. She couldn't be more surprised if the door had been opened by the country's former president.

"Hidalia! How could you have gotten here faster than . . ." But Martha doesn't finish her sentence because she sees that the woman, although similar in appearance to Hidalia (she, too, has an unsubtle mustache), isn't Hidalia.

"Hidalia," says the woman, "is my sister. I am Gisela."

"Oh," Martha says, and she finds herself spilling her sudden fear: "Are you Sergio's wife?"

"No," Gisela says, shaking her head. "I am only his *novia*. But soon, God willing, we will be married."

Gisela looks at Martha carefully, although not with her sister's hard, accusing stare. "You are the American reporter?"

Martha nods.

"Sergio said you would be coming—perhaps last night, perhaps tonight, perhaps tomorrow night. He left you something. Come in."

Martha enters the familiar hallway as Gisela excuses herself. "Here," Gisela says on her return, handing her an envelope.

The note inside is written in English in large, careful letters: "Whenever you need information, I am at service to you. I will never forget our days together." What follows is crossed out, and Martha lifts the page toward the light bulb to read it, but she is unable to. The letter ends, "Good-bye and great luck, Sergio."

She suspects that Sergio is in the apartment, probably in his bedroom under the wool blanket. Or he might be listening at his bedroom door. If she were bold, she would uncover him in his hiding place and overwhelm his injured pride with her apologies, entreaties and kisses. Perhaps he was offering her this very opening in what he crossed out in his letter. Surely, he couldn't have expected or wanted things to finish like this, with a peaceful passing of all she had to Gisela.

Although Gisela is less imposing than her sister, she lifts her shoulders like a bodyguard, determined, it seems, to hold her ground. Martha knows she could move past her with a few quick steps or outflank her by feigning having to use the bathroom. She could even barrel over her, if necessary. Sometime soon, when she is sitting on her balcony in Buenos Aires overlooking the beautiful, lonely city, she will curse, on breath made honest from whiskey, her refusal to surrender her romantic notion of herself and fight, as women and men must sometimes do—with loose emotion, with tears of desire—for companionship, for love.

Now, playing the part she assigned herself long ago, she looks around, noting the details of the apartment one last time—its pine floors, its faded orange and blue cotton rugs, its unadorned, gray walls—and in her mind, she begins writing the story, tapping on the invisible keys she feels beneath her fingers. Somewhere in the lead there is this cool, reasoned summation: "Thankfully, no blood was shed."

In the hotel restaurant the next morning, Martha notices the older American couple. This time, they spot her, and they wave her over to join them. She doesn't demur—she's glad for the company.

She asks about their trip to see the temples, but they hurry through their stories because they are eager to hear hers.

"Tell us," the man says. "Please, tell us what happened."

Even before Martha opens her mouth, the woman claps and exclaims, "How exciting! How very exciting!"

And Martha, the foreign correspondent, tells them how exciting it was and is.

Upon landing in La Paz to begin a trip they hope will help them say a last good-bye to their son, Arnold shocks Jane with his theory: Jeffrey discovered something significant about the drug trade in Bolivia and was preparing to write about it. Whoever would have been exposed by the story wanted him dead, and they either made his death seem self-induced or bribed the Bolivian doctor who performed the autopsy to lie about the cause. In La Paz, Arnold buys a tape recorder and begins secretly to record everyone he speaks with.

Eight days later, at a desk in their hotel room in Coroico, Arnold is completing his transcriptions. In pursuit of what Jane knew from the beginning was a sad, futile attempt to give Jeffrey's death meaning, he has interviewed everyone from the deputy United States ambassador to the store owner in Coroico who said he sold a bottle of water to Jeffrey on the day he died.

Arnold's left hand rests on the tape recorder, his index finger alternately pushing the play and pause button. His right hand is busy scribbling what he's hearing onto yellow legal paper. Periodically during their trip, Jane has tried to pry him from his misguided undertaking. This time, she doesn't bother. "I'm going for a walk," she announces.

Arnold doesn't turn around but lifts his writing hand, the pen still in it, and waves it over his head in a pair of quick, dismissive strikes.

Outside, the late afternoon light is a pale amber color. As Jane walks up the hill toward the center of town, she sees to her right a lush, green valley cradling a river and, beyond it, two snowcapped mountains looming aloof but protective over the landscape. Given such vistas, Jane understands why Jeffrey wanted to come to South America. His plan was to travel by bus from Panama City to Tierra del Fuego. He intended to write a series of essays on the places he saw and the people he met, and he hoped to sell them to newspapers and travel magazines.

It wasn't an unrealistic ambition. After he'd finished a sixty-day treatment program at the Chesapeake Bay Clinic, he began writing movie and concert reviews for the *City Paper* and reported on high school wrestling meets and volleyball matches for *The Washington Post*. Because he was living rent-free at home, he managed to save enough money to fund his trip. He'd been gone three weeks when she and Arnold received a phone call from the designated bad-news bearer at the State Department. Canadian hitchhikers had discovered Jeffrey's body in a cove of dwarf trees outside of Coroico, a town six hours north-northeast of La Paz. The Bolivian doctor, recommended by the U.S. Embassy, said Jeffrey's death was the result of cardiac arrest, abetted by cocaine use. Jane and Arnold paid a large sum to have Jeffrey's body flown home, and they'd buried him in a cemetery across from his high school in clothes Jane found in his closet—blue jeans and a familiar red cashmere sweater.

Before the town square is in view, she hears what sounds like the roars and grunts of racecars. She thinks she must be mistaken, but when she crests the hill, she spots them. She wouldn't exactly call them racecars—they bear little resemblance to what might line the field at the Indianapolis 500—but they are clearly intended to race. They all have souped-up engines and numbers painted on their doors and hoods. Some even have sponsor logos, the most popular of which is Paceña, Bolivia's national beer, which seems to hold the allegiance of half the field. The collection of cars is what a person might find at a used auto dealership: Ford Mustangs, Toyota Corollas, even two original VW Beetles.

Jane steps into a small crowd surrounding one of the nicer looking cars. It's a Mercedes, probably from the late seventies. It is painted red, white, and blue and its name is written in large black cursive letters across the hood: *El Gringo*.

To a boy standing on his toes next her, Jane asks in her slow, precise Spanish, "When is the race?"

"Tomorrow at noon."

"Where are they racing?"

"To La Paz."

"La Paz?" Jane asks with surprise. To get from La Paz to Coroico, she and Arnold drove their rented Camry on a road Jane could only imagine was designed by someone with a death wish. The predominantly single-lane, dirt road had only a tenuous relationship with the Cordillera Real mountain range. During some stretches, it seemed to veer off into the air, as if the road's designer had counted on low-lying clouds to keep vehicles from plunging over the rail-less edge. As they traversed one particularly narrow stretch, she said to her husband, "Drive slowly, Honey, or Jeffrey will have our company sooner than we want." She hoped the remark would make light of the heaviness they were both feeling, but it had come out wrong, and Arnold neither responded nor slowed down.

The road is the only one from Coroico to La Paz, and she can't believe anyone would be crazy enough to race on it. One false turn of the wheel, one overeager run to pass in one of the few stretches where two cars could fit on the road simultaneously, one instance of tapping the gas pedal instead of the brake . . . .

"I don't see how . . . ," Jane begins to tell the boy, but he is gone, following the crowd to another Mercedes painted in bright colors—the red, green, and white of the Mexican flag—at the end of the square. Its engine revs like an airplane's, and the crowd shouts in delight.

Jane finds herself directly in front of the *El Gringo* Mercedes. A young man in an orange jumpsuit—he looks like a Bolivian astronaut—is leaning against the driver-side door. He is as short as Jane and wears his thick black hair long. A cross earring glints in his left ear, a companion to the larger cross around his neck. He has been looking at his shoes, but when Jane is in front of him he lifts his head and smiles.

"Hello," she says, speaking English because of the car's name.

The Bolivian says, "Hello." Even with this lone word, she can hear how heavy his accent is.

She continues in Spanish, "Usted es el piloto?"

He smiles in apparent appreciation of her use of Spanish and answers in English, "Yes." He nods toward the Mercedes. "I am driver. My name is Geronimo."

He looks no older than twenty-five, although Jane knows how deceptive appearances can be with Latin Americans. One of the secretaries in the National Gallery, where Jane is the associate curator, is from Nicaragua, and Jane always thought she was in her late forties until she announced her retirement the previous month at age sixty-two.

"You have a nice car," Jane tells him.

"Thank you," he says. "I bought it in United States."

"Did you live in the States?"

"Four years. Texas. I worked in a bank. Dallas, Texas. I save money to buy the car."

"It's an expensive car," Jane says.

"Yes. Expensive. Used car, but expensive. But I have no wife, no children. Only my mother. I give her some money. The rest is for me."

"Have you been racing long?"

"This my second race. The last race, in Copacabana, I finish . . . ." He holds up four fingers. "I finish four. Tomorrow, I want finish . . . ." He holds up his index finger.

"In first place," Jane says.

"First place."

"I don't understand how . . . ." Jane begins, wanting to ask about the impossible and frightening road to La Paz. She pauses to reconsider how to phrase her question. "The road to La Paz is difficult." She gestures with her hand to illustrate the severity of the mountain slope. "If I were driving, I would be scared."

Geronimo nods passionately and says, "Yes, yes, yes. My mother tell me what you tell me. Very . . . ." He makes the same gesture she made. "But here in Bolivia, roads are . . . *así.*"

"Aren't you scared?"

Geronimo touches the cross on his chest. "I have God." He mispronounces the next word, but she understands it: *Protection.*

"Is racing cars your profession?" she asks him.

"If I win . . . ," he begins. He says the next few sentences in Spanish: "If I win, I can earn good money. But there are many men who want to win. I have saved enough money to become a racecar driver. Even if I do not win this year, I will be all right. But if I do not win next year, I will return to the United States to work."

"Does your mother live here?"

"In La Paz."

"She must miss you when you go to the United States."

"Yes," Geronimo says in English. "She miss me." His cross earring glimmers in the fading light.

The sounds of revving engines are all around them. She can hear excited conversations from the crowds of people gathered in the square.

"Your family is in United States?" he asks.

"My husband is here with me. I have three children." She is conscious immediately of her mistake, of keeping Jeffrey in the present tense.

"Why you come to Bolivia?" he asks.

"My son was here," Jane says. "He's a writer. He was writing a story about Bolivia."

"Yes," Geronimo says, nodding. "Beautiful country."

"He has a sense of adventure—like you."

"We have adventure." He curls his right hand into a fist and swings it in front of his chest like a symphony conductor. "We are . . . how do you say . . . 'sin miedo'?"

"Without fear," she says. "Fearless."

"Fearless," he repeats, smiling. "Your son, I, we are fearless."

Jeffrey might, at times, have been fearless, she thinks, but she never did anything but fear for him. When he was a boy, he often came down with flues and fevers, a couple of them severe enough to require trips to the hospital. And when he was a teenager, she worried about his drinking and drug use. If the phone rang late at night, she was sure it would be someone calling to tell her Jeffrey was dead. She sustained her worry even after he completed his stay at the Chesapeake Bay Clinic, the most lengthy and costly of his drug abuse treatments, and assured her and Arnold that he was, at last, clean.

Sometimes even now, a month after his death, she finds herself worrying about him. It isn't a conscious worry, only a gnawing, familiar weight in her stomach. It's as if he is still vulnerable to pain, misfortune, the destructive temptations of loneliness, and by offering him her breast, her arms, her reassuring words, she could put the world, for a moment or two, at peace for him.

"When you have children," she says to Geronimo, "you will be less fearless."

"Yes," he says. "And if I fall off mountain . . . ." Grinning, he swoops his hand down from his shoulder. "I will be less fearless."

She tries to laugh, which is clearly the response he wants, but she feels a tightening in her stomach. She wants to tell him, as she did her husband: Drive slowly. But she doesn't know him—and, besides, the advice would be absurd to a racecar driver—so she can only give him a forced chuckle.

He seems to sense her unease because he frowns. And as if he knew her, as if he knew what she was thinking, he says, "No worry. I drive like . . . like . . . ." He scrunches up his eyes in contemplation, then spills the name with relief: "Like Andretti!"

"Good," she says, and she finds herself reaching for his shoulder, the way she does with people she knows. She catches herself, however, and her hand hangs in the air as if she were about to bless him.

Quickly, yet with grace, Geronimo takes her hand between both of his. She is surprised by how soft and small his hands are, a child's hands. "Nice," he says, "to meet you."

Jane climbs a hill on the east side of town and enters the *calvario*. No one is inside. A handful of candles burn at the altar. She lingers a minute in front of the gruesome statue of Christ—His mouth is contorted, as if He has swallowed something bitter, and His blue eyes reflect the opposite of resignation—before stepping outside and sitting on a bench with a view of the town.

She wonders if Jeffrey came here, and decides he probably didn't. He never liked being by himself. When he was a little boy, a year or two old, and she'd leave him alone even for a minute—to answer the phone, to retrieve her purse from the car—he would cry, a deep, piercing wail that seemed to come from a place too profound and dark for someone so young. When he was a teenager, he attached himself to boys who seemed to consider Jeffrey half a companion and half an experiment to see how much they could abuse him while keeping his friendship. One day, he came home with two burn marks on his back, and, when she pressed him, he confessed that his friend Steven had wanted to see how flesh reacted when singed by cigarettes. She and Arnold forbade Jeffrey to see Steven again, but she knew he disobeyed her because she saw Steven under Jeffrey's window one night, throwing rocks at it like a lover.

In college, Jeffrey fell in with a crowd of older men and women who were at one time full-time students but had failed to graduate and maintained only a peripheral connection to the university. Jeffrey, too, never graduated, and she and Arnold blamed it on his restlessness—he always wanted to be somewhere else.

The day after Jeffrey left on his trip, she and Arnold sat in the living room with pre-dinner glasses of Chardonnay, and Arnold said, "This time, I think he knows exactly what he's doing." She wanted to ratify his belief in Jeffrey. She tried to—she tried to smile, to breathe easily—but Arnold recognized her counterfeit response and downed his wine with haste, as if swallowing his hope.

Night settles over Coroico like a blue blanket being woven slowly from the cool air. She doesn't want to leave in the morning, as they have planned. She wants, at dawn, to find a high spot, higher than where she is now, and follow Geronimo around the mountain's curves.

It is dark when she climbs down the hill. In a house on her left, a dog barks. She flinches, but the sound comes no closer.

In the town square, the lights are ablaze. It's as bright as noon. Purposely, she walks on the opposite side of the street from Geronimo. She sees him standing in front of his Mercedes in his astronaut costume. Half a dozen children surround him, pestering him for autographs. When he looks up, she thinks he sees her, and she waves. Less than twenty yards separate them, but he fails to notice her, and he drops his head to sign another autograph.

She remembers seeing Jeffrey from a similar distance after the last night of his high school play. He'd been Tom in *The Glass Menagerie*, and he'd played the part with humor and a sweet sentimentality she'd never seen in him. Members of the audience, composed of students and their parents, came afterwards to congratulate him, shaking his hand or, in the case of a pair of girls, holding on to his shoulder and whispering in his ear. It was as if they wanted to touch what he'd created, the vividness he'd given the dreamer, Tom. It was the first time Jane had seen Jeffrey like this, confident, appreciated, and she felt a rush of gratitude—for the drama teacher for having selected Jeffrey for the part, for Tennessee Williams for having written such a beautiful play, for the world itself, which seemed, at last, to have embraced her son, welcomed him without cruelty.

When he didn't try out for the school's spring production, she asked him why, and he'd given her a shrug and an evasive answer. She'd intended to follow up on it, to press him, but she hadn't. The moment was swept up in other moments. It was a busy time.

She watches Geronimo finish his autographs and lean back against his car. He folds his hands across his chest and gazes at the sky. He looks vigorous, assured, as if he's posing for a photograph, the great racer on the night before the big race.

If she could have one power, it would be to slow time, to allow moments of triumph and contentment to stretch years. But how quickly after such occasions one finds oneself on the mountain's edge, staring over the side at ruin and eternity.

From outside their hotel room on the second floor, she smells a faint, acrid odor. It is a more bitter and unpleasant smell than cigarettes, which Arnold, despite being a doctor, occasionally indulges in. Entering the room, she doesn't see Arnold sitting at the desk in the corner, as she anticipated, nor is he napping on the bed. The smell is stronger here. Worried, she calls his name.

He is in the bathroom, kneeling over the toilet. The burning smell is thick, and she coughs. "Have you set a fire in here?" she asks him.

He looks up. It's obvious he has been crying. His eyes are red and his thin, gray hair is tangled and standing on end.

She feels a familiar urge to put her hands on his shoulders, comfort him. But a part of her is still engaged with what is outside their hotel, with Geronimo and his revved-up Mercedes. All the way back to the hotel in the growing dark, she worried about Geronimo and the terrible road. Several times, she stopped, thinking: I'll go back and tell him to be careful.

Arnold begins to laugh, and his laughter resonates in the small, tiled bathroom. His laughter disturbs her because it is far from joyous. Nevertheless, she senses in it a hint of relief.

"I finished transcribing the tapes," he says and laughs again.

He doesn't say more, and to fill the silence, she says, "That's good, Arnold. When we're in La Paz tomorrow, we can look over the transcripts." She isn't being condescending; after her conversation with Geronimo, she decided she was too quick to see Jeffrey's death as his final, weak succumbing to his addiction. Jeffrey deserves more from her than this, and perhaps with scrutiny, she would find in the transcripts something to save him from the indignity of a death by overdose—or at least give her permission to doubt, however illogically, the official explanation.

"We won't be reading over the transcripts," he says. "The last one's here." He taps the seat of the toilet and stands up.

"What do you mean?" she asks.

"I burned every stupid, inconsequential word." He looks at himself in the wide mirror above the sink and pats down his hair. "I don't think I've done so much meaningless writing since I copied the entire entry on Alabama from the *Encyclopedia Britannica* for a report in my fifth-grade geography class."

"You burned them all?" she asks uneasily.

He nods, taking a step toward her.

"Arnold, we spent the whole week interviewing people about Jeffrey, and you spent all of last night and all of today transcribing what they'd said, and . . . ."

"No one said anything, Jane." He speaks in a low, quiet voice—his soothing doctor's voice. "I mean, no one said anything to contradict what we know. They said a whole lot about themselves." He tries to smile. "About the only thing I can say for the experience is that I brushed up on my Spanish." He pauses. "And maybe I said another good-bye to Jeffrey."

"You could have saved them," she says, and she feels anger rise in her voice. "You could have saved them for me."

"For you?" he asks. "Sweetheart, you were the one who thought I was crazy for . . . ." He breaks off. She wishes he would finish—they might have an argument. They haven't argued since Jeffrey died. Instead, they've become cautious with each other, as if their wounds were visible and anything hard, a fierce kiss or angry words, might inflame them.

He gives her his look of professional sympathy, and she wants to lash out against it. But she knows he wouldn't engage her. She takes a deep breath and coughs because of the smoke.

He takes her by the shoulders and leads her gently out of the bathroom.

In La Paz the next day, they eat lunch at Pronto Ristorante and shop at stores off the Plaza Murillo, buying wool sweaters and scarves and mittens for their grandchildren. They eat an early dinner at La Fiesta, sharing a cheese and sausage pizza. It is already half dark when they leave the restaurant. The air is cold and they're underdressed. Jane is tempted to wear one of the sweaters she bought. Instead, she wraps her forearms around her chest.

On Calle Linares, they pass a series of market stalls, all of them relying on the weak streetlights to illuminate their wares. This is El Mercado de Hechicería, where, according to their guidebook, all the vendors are witches—or at least are supposed to sell magic potions.

Jane looks at one vendor, a woman whose dark eyes have receded into her wrinkled face. They seem to stare out at Jane as if from a cave. "*Qué quiere, señora?*" the woman asks her, pointing to what is spread on her wooden cart.

Jane takes a step toward the woman. "Is that . . . ," she begins to ask, and when she understands what she's looking at, she can't hold back her disgust. "My God!" Jane says, backing up. "My God!"

Arnold is several paces ahead of her. Having heard her, he comes quickly to her side. "What?"

"Terrible," she says.

"What is?"

"That!" she says, gesturing behind her as she walks away. She knows she is acting childish, boorish even. She isn't a typical tourist. She has always appreciated a range of cultural beliefs and practices; anyone in the arts does—or should. But what is on the woman's cart has unnerved her, and she can't pretend otherwise. She wants to leave. But Arnold isn't coming, and she is forced to stop at the end of the street and wait for him. She keeps her eyes focused on the sky, worried about what she might see elsewhere.

A minute later, Arnold catches up with her. "The llama fetus?" he asks her.

"Could we go, please? Please, could we go?"

"All right," he says, and they walk in silence toward their hotel.

At the door of the Hotel Radisson Plaza, Arnold says, "Llama fetuses are considered sacred. When Bolivians build a new home, they bury a fetus beneath the foundation."

"Okay," she tells him. "All right."

To the right of the lobby is the hotel's restaurant and bar, and as they're walking toward the bank of elevators, Jane stops to stare at the image on the bar's television: a car sailing off the edge of a mountain. Her heart fires against her chest, and she turns again to Arnold, but he has gone ahead of her, pushing the elevator button.

She rushes into the bar, which is empty, and approaches the bartender, a tall, pale man with large eyes.

"What is this?" she asks, gesturing toward the television screen. "Is this the race today? Is this the race from Coroico?"

Already, she can tell it isn't. Credits have begun to roll over a shot of the car in midair.

The bartender's English is slow and clear: "It is called *Thelma and Louise*. It is a movie you know?"

"No," she says, distracted. "I mean, yes. Yes, I've seen it." Her heart, however, doesn't slow down. If anything it is beating faster. Perhaps the movie's ending is an omen, she thinks, a foretaste of what she'll soon learn about the race.

How could she have been so cruel, so selfish as to leave Coroico without giving Geronimo a last warning? If something happened to him, it will be her fault, and she'll never forgive herself. "Listen," she says, turning with urgency to the bartender. "Listen. Did you hear about the race today, the race from Coroico?"

"A race from Coroico?" he asks, smiling his puzzlement.

"A car race," she says. "Automobiles."

"I don't know of a car race in Coroico."

"It was from Coroico to La Paz, to here," she says, pounding the bar's counter as if it were the finish line. "Today."

"No," he says. "I heard nothing."

"How could I find out about it?" Then, her voice rising, she says, "I need to know."

"Yes. All right. Let me see." He puts a finger on his lower lip and taps it several times. In the meantime, Arnold has come up to her. He asks her if she's all right.

She doesn't respond. She is waiting for the bartender to give her an answer.

"Certainly, the news . . . ," he begins. "But on channel six, the . . . how do you say it . . . the picture is a little . . . "

"It's okay," she says. "Let's watch the news."

The bartender reaches to turn the channel. As he warned, the picture is fuzzy, but she sees well enough to be satisfied. To Arnold, she explains what she is hoping to learn. Sighing, he sits down next to her. Several times he looks at her with concern. His glances annoy her. Finally, she says, "Order yourself a drink."

"I think I will," he says. "Do you want one?"

"No."

The bartender leaves to bring Arnold his beer, and she is worried that in his absence, news of the race will come on. Jane doesn't understand much of what the anchorwoman is saying, although now she must be talking about what happened in Mexico because a map of the country is illuminated behind her.

The bartender returns with Arnold's beer.

"I need help," Jane tells the bartender, "understanding what they're saying. When they talk about the race—please—tell me what they're saying."

"Of course," the bartender says.

But the woman on the screen talks about Russia and China and the United States. She talks about Paraguay and Argentina.

"Is this some kind of international station?" Jane asks the bartender.

"No," he says. "It is from Bolivia."

And then the screen shows a long stretch of black road and cars racing on it. The TV woman is speaking over the sound of roaring engines. "What is she saying?" Jane pleads.

"She is talking about the race," the bartender says with an animated wave of his right hand.

The screen shows the winner, a man with a narrow face and long ears, celebrating by holding up a trophy. Behind him, she is gratified and relieved to see Geronimo. He keeps bobbing his head, as if hoping to be part of the picture.

"There he is!" she yells.

"Yes," the bartender says. "The winner, Francisco García, the Mexican."

"No, behind him," she says. "Behind him!"

"Who?" the bartender asks, but already the screen shows a soccer game—a booming kick, a flailing goalie.

She turns to Arnold, who has slipped off his barstool. "He's all right," she tells him. "Thank God, he's all right."

She puts her arms around her husband and pulls him to her. Smelling the beer on his breath and the sweat and deodorant from his body, she remembers how, when she reached Jeffrey after his high school play and embraced him in congratulations, he smelled of make-up and hair spray and the faint mildew from the old navy coat he was wearing. She drew back, surprised by his strange odor, but as quickly hugged him again, hugged him because this was all she could do and all she wanted to do.

She is reassured by the thought of herself holding him in whatever costume he is assembled, however unfamiliar the ways in which he reaches her senses.

"He's all right," she says, surprised and relieved to be crying.

"I'm glad," Arnold says, pressing his lips into her hair. "I'm very glad."

The pilot has announced that they are sixty miles south of the Cleveland airport, and for the first time since leaving Guatemala, Kelly permits herself to feel relieved. Relieved means sighing. Relieved means smiling. She turns toward Manuel, whose nose is pressed against the window. "You're mine now," she mouths to the back of his head.

She is returning home after three years in the Peace Corps and is bringing with her the man she married two months ago. They are about to begin new lives in a place that will be perhaps slightly different to her but completely foreign to him. She worried he would have doubts about leaving his country and family, doubts about being with her for the rest of his life. But so far he has remained the same Manuel, smiling when she looks at him, taking her hand sometimes, making an occasional comment about what strikes him as odd or exciting. ("Se puede usar el teléfono en el aire?" he asked her, fingering the telephone in the seatback pocket in front of her.) Clearing customs in Miami was a first hurdle. He could have panicked, been overcome with the significance of what he was doing. But he smiled the entire time they waited in the long line, and when they had gone through, he welcomed her to her own country with the flourish of a tour guide.

At the airport, Kelly is expecting to meet her mother, uncle, aunt, and grandmother. She has not seen them since she left for Guatemala, three months after she graduated from Cleveland State, a degree she paid for by working full-time at an agricultural supply warehouse off Route 77. Too poor and provincial (no one but her uncle has been out of Ohio in the last five years), they didn't come to her wedding in Guatemala, a small ceremony presided over by the mayor of San Cristóbal, the town where she lived. Kelly and Manuel are, however, planning a second wedding in the St. Ignatius Church in Cleveland. Everyone in her family will be there, except her father, whom she hasn't seen since she was twelve.

Kelly's family is not exactly excited about having Manuel as an in-law. When, over the bad connection in the Guatel office in San Cristóbal, Kelly told them about her engagement, the best her grandmother could shout across the static-filled line was "at least he's Catholic." Kelly hopes time has softened their displeasure. She needs them as allies. She wants them to make Manuel feel welcome.

"*Cinco minutos mas*," Kelly tells Manuel when she hears the wheels sprouting under the plane. He looks at her. Is he paler than usual? She takes his hand. Is it trembling a little? He smiles. His face is the same dark brown. His hand is warm, smooth and still.

She feels the plane fall and, in the window behind her husband, sees they have gone below the clouds. Cleveland is spread below them in a midsummer haze. She sees cars, small rectangles of blue, green, white and red, running up and down Interstate 71. Or is it Interstate 480? No matter. She's home.

She pulls her bag from the overhead bin—it's a blue, purple and white knapsack made of Guatemalan fabric. She grabs Manuel's backpack. Although made in Guatemala, it sports a Chicago Bulls logo on the top flap. Kelly tried to explain to him that the Bulls aren't popular in Cleveland, having beaten the Cavaliers several times in the playoffs, but Manuel only shrugged and said, "They are my favorite team." She didn't argue. And handing the backpack to him, she figures it will make a good conversation piece. Her uncle, a basketball fan, has a partial season ticket plan for the Cavaliers.

Kelly leads them off the plane, down the ramp, and into the waiting area, where she sees her uncle standing at the entrance with his wife and two daughters, who hold up a sign: *Welcome Home, Kelly*. Thoughtfully, someone—Kelly decides it must be Aunt Ellen—has added, in smaller letters and a different color, + *Manuel*. Against the wall behind the check-in counter, Kelly spots her mother and grandmother, and they wave. Kelly feels her heart pound rapidly, but the introductions and the exchanges of hugs and kisses are over quickly, and Kelly pulls in a good deep breath. Home, she thinks.

Soon, they are marching toward the baggage claim area. Kelly's uncle, Vince, a heavy-set man whose close-cropped hair has turned completely gray in her absence, has taken notice of Manuel's backpack. "So you're a Bulls fan?" he asks.

Manuel knows perhaps ten words in English, and Bulls is one of them, so he is able to repeat it forcefully.

"Don't say that too loud around here," Vince says. "It might get you into trouble." Vince smiles and Manuel copies him.

"What did I tell you?" Kelly whispers in Spanish, and Manuel acknowledges her prophecy with a shrug and another smile.

"We are looking forward to your wedding," Kelly's grandmother tells her. "Father McGuane had planned to go on vacation, but when he heard you wanted to be married in late July, he postponed it. He's so proud of you, Kelly, and what you did in Guatemala." She turns to Manuel and says loudly, "It's a very nice church."

Manuel nods, although Kelly knows he hasn't understood anything. Quickly, Kelly translates and he says, "Yes. Good."

Manuel is looking around swiftly, as if not wanting to miss any of the sights around him. She imagines it must be for him both exciting and overwhelming. She tries to catch his glance, to share with him the newness of his environment, but he isn't looking at her.

They have to wait a few minutes before their bags tumble off the conveyor belt. Standing beside Manuel, Kelly is for the first time in months aware of the height difference between them. Maybe it's the little sunburned, red-haired girl who keeps staring at them from behind her mother's skirt that makes Kelly self-conscious. Kelly is almost six feet tall and Manuel is barely five feet, six inches. She is also wider than Manuel. Her mother always called her "big-boned" when she was growing up, although some of her classmates were less charitable. She didn't lose weight in Guatemala as she'd hoped. Manuel, however, has always praised her body, even away from the bedroom, and his courtship of her seemed like a continuous seduction. Whether they were building latrines together or downing a six-pack of Gallo in the living room of her house in San Cristóbal, he seemed to look at her as if she were half clothed. He has made her feel perpetually desirable. She wonders, though, if her relatives are like the red-haired girl and see her and Manuel as a freak couple, tall, fat and pale teaming up with short, slim and dark.

She has brought four bags, two over the limit, a privilege for which she had to pay an extra $75. Manuel, though, hasn't packed much; all his clothes and everything else he couldn't stuff into his Bulls backpack are contained in a medium-sized imitation leather suitcase, which he carries without straining. Uncle Vince has gone to retrieve his mini-van, and they wait for him outside.

Uncle Vince's two daughters, a decade younger than Kelly, are whispering to each other. Both are blond-haired and thin, and Kelly has always envied them. At family gatherings at her uncle's house, relatives always praised their beauty with exclamations —"Aren't they the prettiest pair you've ever seen!"—and reserved for Kelly strained approval of her hardworking nature.

When her father left, Kelly and her mother moved in with Uncle Vince and his family. While Uncle Vince, too, liked to salute her hard work in public, he found several private occasions to ask her, always with a certain smile, if she'd ever had a boyfriend and once, in apparent seriousness, said it would be "all right" with him if she were a lesbian, even if he didn't think it would be a "big hit" with the rest of the family.

Kelly hears Manuel whisper something into her ear, and she is not sure what he's said. Lost in reverie, she finds the Spanish strange and out of place. When she figures out what he has told her, he is already making his way through the automatic glass doors and back into the airport. She thinks to tell him to leave his bags with her, but it's too late.

"What's wrong?" Aunt Ellen asks her, and Kelly feels the entire family crowding around her.

Is their faith in her marriage this fragile? she wonders. Do they expect a crisis the minute after she and Manuel have arrived? She tries to laugh, make a joke about Manuel's small bladder, but the words get tangled somehow and finally she can only blurt out the fact: "He went to the bathroom."

Uncle Vince pulls up in his silver Dodge minivan. Aunt Ellen slides open the door and her daughters climb in first, staking out the back seat. Aunt Ellen follows. Maria, Kelly's mother, whispers, "He's very handsome." Kelly thanks her. This, at least, is encouraging.

"Where's Pedro?" Uncle Vince shouts. Aunt Ellen hisses "Manuel" at him, and he smiles. "Right, right," he says, hardly repentant. Kelly hoped Uncle Vince would support her decision to marry Manuel (it would, anyway, disprove his lesbian theory) or at least remain neutral, but there is something derisive in his apparent forgetfulness. Kelly looks to her mother for support. Although Maria recently moved out of Uncle Vince's house and into an apartment in East Cleveland, she has never been good at standing up to her brother. She smiles wanly.

After another minute, her mother says, "Maybe he's lost."

Kelly wonders if this is an implied criticism, if her mother is suggesting Manuel is too stupid to find his way back from the bathroom. She is angry at her family and angry, too, at Manuel, who is probably dawdling in the men's room, laying on the pink liquid soap and keeping his hands a long time under the hot water. There is no hot water in the faucets in Guatemala, not, anyway, in places Manuel has ever been.

Kelly says, "I'll go get him," and she is glad to be away, however briefly, from the cramped minivan. She walks through the glass doors and follows the sign to the bathroom past the Continental and Southwest ticket counters. She walks down a flight of stairs and stands in front of the door to the men's room, where four men in business suits and one with rumpled hair and torn blue jeans exit. She wonders if she should ask someone on his way in to call out Manuel's name. She has half a mind to step into the bathroom herself. But after a few more men leave, she decides Manuel must have gone to another bathroom. Or perhaps he went to this bathroom and, their paths having crossed on opposite staircases, is already back in front of the terminal, already in Uncle Vince's van.

She walks back up the stairs and looks out the large glass windows to where the minivan is. Her mother is still waiting on the curb, and she has been joined by Aunt Ellen.

Kelly marches past the Southwest and Continental counters again toward Concourse A, where she figures there also must be a bathroom. She finds one there and watches a dozen men leave. Her heart begins to race again.

She concludes that Manuel is probably sitting on the toilet in the first bathroom she visited, constipated or having a bout of diarrhea. She has heard stories about Peace Corps volunteers having trouble readjusting to the rich food and chlorinated water of the States. In Manuel's case, though, it's probably simply nerves. She waits another minute in front of the Concourse A bathroom, then again passes the Southwest and Continental counters and turns toward the Concourse B bathroom.

Her mother is standing in front of it, biting her lower lip. She sees Kelly and manages a half smile. "Takes his time, doesn't he?" she asks.

Kelly explains her theory about Manuel's nervousness. "Of course," she says, nodding a little too vigorously. Kelly has always resented her mother's lack of confidence in her. Maria didn't think Kelly could hold down a full-time job and go to college at the same time. (Maria didn't have the money to pay for Kelly's education, however, and Uncle Vince never volunteered to help.) She didn't think Kelly should join the Peace Corps because Guatemala was a long way away and "something bad" might happen to her. When Kelly learned that her mother had moved out of Uncle Vince's house, she thought it might be a sign that her mother was changing, growing stronger and more independent. But if her mother has undergone such a transformation, she isn't showing any signs of it. She is the mother Kelly has always been a little ashamed of.

A minute passes. Kelly turns and sees Uncle Vince enter through the automatic doors and look around. She despises him and doesn't want him to see her, not until they find Manuel.

"Maybe he locked himself in a stall," Maria says. "I read about this guy spending the night in a bathroom in Cleveland Stadium. Couldn't get out of the john, and by the time he did, everyone had gone home and all the exits were locked. He ended up going down on the field, pretending he was Lou Boudreau and swinging at imaginary fastballs."

"Oh, Mom," Kelly says, only half listening. "Please."

When Uncle Vince arrives, Maria says, "Will you go into the bathroom and see if Kelly's husband is around?" Uncle Vince nods and sidesteps a man in a blue business suit who's on his way out. Inside Kelly hears him shout, "Pedro!" and something icy goes through her, half anger and half terror that she is being mocked for her decision to marry a Guatemalan farmer, a man who didn't finish eighth grade. She thinks of how delighted Uncle Vince was when her father left them. Her father had worked for a shipping company and Uncle Vince's joke, repeated whenever the occasion suited him, was that he'd mailed himself to "Irresponsibility, U.S.A."

She turns furiously to her mother. "His name is Manuel! Mom, his name is Manuel!"

Her mother blushes. Uncle Vince's vigorous "Pedro? Pedro?" is ringing throughout the bathroom, and Maria moves to the entrance, tailing a tall, bald guy in loafers and a purple golf shirt, and calls out, "His name is Manuel, Vince. His name is Manuel!"

As Kelly is waiting, her right foot tapping against the floor, she recalls the conversation she had with Manuel the previous night. It concerned the money she had been given by the Peace Corps. Of her $5600 readjustment allowance, she had asked for $2000 in cash. She had a job lined up teaching Spanish at St. Mary's High School for Girls in the fall, and she wanted to find an apartment for herself and Manuel immediately. It would be a few days, she figured, before she got around to opening a bank account, and she wanted to be able to have enough cash on hand to pay two months' rent. She anticipated being overwhelmed by her family and was hoping she and Manuel would have to stay in her uncle's house for only a day or two.

She told Manuel about the cash, and he insisted on seeing the money. She showed it to him, his first contact, so far as she knew, with U.S. dollars, an almost mythical currency in Guatemala. "I will carry the money," he said.

She laughed at him, thinking he was joking. When she saw he wasn't, she asked, "Why?"

"Like you said, from the day of our wedding, we are sharing everything. Our lives, our futures. And our money. Or were you lying?"

She shook her head.

"I will need to be responsible for some things, and I will start with the money." Then he added, almost plaintively, "Please."

She wondered if she was running up against something cultural, if his machismo, however controlled it had been during his wooing of her, was resurfacing. She knew this had the potential to lead to a nasty fight, fierce words she didn't want, not the night before going home, so she gave in and even smiled when she handed him the bills.

He showed her where he was putting them, in his wallet, shoved deep in his front pocket. "*Muy seguro*," he said, patting his wallet protectively.

When her mother turns away from the bathroom and looks at her with a false smile, she feels like crying, admitting her stupidity. She has been played, her sentiments tapped like the keys of a marimba, He convinced her she was pretty when she was ugly, convinced her he wanted her when all he wanted was a ticket to the States and a wallet full of dollars. *Son of a bitch*, she wants to scream.

Her mother is apologizing for her uncle, saying he has always had problems with names. And soon he is calling "Manuel! Manuel!" with aplomb.

Her two cousins join Kelly and her mother, chewing gum and looking bored. "Maybe he forgot something on the plane," says one of her cousins. "Yeah," says the other, giggling a little. "Maybe his sombrero." Kelly doesn't know if they are ignorant or mean—she figures the latter. She guesses they are both sick of hearing, at every family gathering, about Kelly's wonderful work in Guatemala. During her absence, Kelly has been perfect. Meanwhile, her cousins both flunked classes in high school.

Uncle Vince comes out of the bathroom. "I guarantee you there is no one by the name of Manuel in there—or Pedro." Uncle Vince's laughter booms, and Kelly is grateful that her cousins think themselves too cool to join in.

Kelly bows her head, stares at her tennis shoes, still dusted lightly with Guatemalan soil. She wonders how long it will take for the dust to come off. She might be carrying molecules of Guatemala around with her for months, insignificant crumbs of a life she'd loved. She realizes, with something resembling panic, that she is no longer home—she is only back at home.

She begins, softly, to cry, hoping no one sees her. She wipes her eyes, trying frantically to stop her tears. She wants to be back in San Cristóbal, sitting in the hammock on her porch, peeling a *mandarina*, watching the sun die above the mountains. And when it's dark, she wants Manuel to come, as he always does, tired from working in his father's field, wants him to come smelling lightly of sweat and dirt, wants him to drink beer with her and tell her she's the most beautiful woman he knows. Feeling sick, she realizes that what they had can only be perfect there. She knows it can't be transplanted in the States amid interstates and boorish and ignorant relatives.

Staring at her shoes, she hears the conversations around her cease. She looks up and sees Manuel strutting out of the entrance to Concourse B. He is looking paler and more concerned than she has ever seen him, and her heart beats frantically, both in relief at finding him and a renewed sense of panic over what's wrong. She takes a step toward him, and her relatives clear a path.

She is about to ask him what happened, but he speaks first: "*Necesito usar el baño.*" She tells him she thought he *was* using the bathroom. He nods, then shakes his head. He tells her he'd gone back to use the bathroom on the plane—he'd used it early in their trip and had raved about it to Kelly—but had been held back by a woman at the counter, who didn't understand him. She called over a friend, who also didn't understand him. He showed them his airline ticket, proving he'd been on the flight, but they didn't want to let him back through the door. They then called over a man, who also didn't understand him. Finally, Manuel gave up.

Kelly laughs, relieved. "Here's the bathroom," she says, pointing.

He thanks her, walks past her relatives and, still carrying his bags, disappears. She would like to follow him, help him through everything in his first day in the United States, even the act of relieving himself, but she knows she must learn to give him the distance he will need to build a new life, however painful the process, and hope that, at nightfall, he isn't too exhausted and too defeated to whisper the words she has come to expect and need from him. If he remembers to speak them, maybe she will be able to endure the humiliation of her family and the strangeness of her country.

She closes her eyes and whispers a prayer, surprising herself with how easily the words come: urgent, hopeful, and all in Spanish.

When Charlie Perkins steps into Lavandería La Merced, Marisol greets him with a gasp. "Oh, Don Carlitos, _lo siento_." She covers her mouth with both of her tiny hands.

Having slept well for the first time in a week, Charlie is in a good mood. "My white shirt?"

"Perdón?"

"Was it my white dress shirt you ruined?"

The four washers and four dryers behind Marisol, a girl of fourteen who looks older, hum and shake. Above the machines is a line of dress shirts: whites and blues, a few browns, a few yellows. "Your shirt," Marisol says, "is finished. Clean."

"Great. So did you lose one of my T-shirts again?" The first time he'd had his wash done here, he'd returned to his apartment two blocks down the street to find his favorite T-shirt—one his wife, Liv, had bought him at a New York Knicks game—missing.

Marisol shakes her head.

"So what is it?" he asks. "What's wrong?"

She waves to him, and it takes him a moment to realize she is inviting him inside. He steps around the counter and follows her past the washers and dryers and into an unlit hallway. At the end is an open door to the courtyard, but they stop short of it and step into a room on the right. Marisol's mother, Doña Aura, is sitting on a worn brown couch in front of a television.

On the screen, Charlie sees the twin towers of the World Trade Center, one in flames, the other about to be struck by an airplane. Now it is struck, and fire explodes from a high floor. An announcer is speaking in Spanish, but Charlie can't understand him above the television's static. The same scene is shown again and a third time before the camera cuts to a man with salt-and-pepper hair sitting behind an anchor's desk.

Charlie turns to Doña Aura. "What happened?" he asks.

She looks up at him, her eyes holding the heavy, vacant glaze of someone who watches too much television. "Your city," she says. "It's gone."

Fifteen minutes later, Charlie is standing at the back of a crowd in Mistral, a gringo bar. The television above the bar is tuned to CNN, but he isn't close enough to hear what's being said.

He feels a hand on his shoulder, and he turns to find Eliza. She's as blond as he is and only two inches shorter, and sometimes when Guatemalans see them together, they ask if they're related. Eliza is from London, and when she tells him what she knows, in a voice too low and measured to indicate ease, he feels as if he's listening to the BBC.

"Both towers?" he asks.

She nods.

He turns back to the television screen. His view is blocked by the dreadlocks of the man in front of him. Charlie cranes his head. "But look—they're still standing," he says. "They're only on fire."

A minute later, he sees what Eliza told him confirmed. The TV shows a replay of first the South Tower, then the North, collapsing. The fifty-person crowd, jammed into a space only a little larger than an average New York City bedroom, murmurs. Directly below the television, a woman begins to sob.

"I'm so sorry," Eliza says. She is, he realizes, still holding him by the shoulder. Although they've slept together, he finds her hand foreign—heavy and with long fingernails that bite into his skin.

"Who did it?" he asks.

"They think terrorists, maybe Osama bin Laden's group," she says. "But they don't know." She pauses before delivering the next line with the same unnatural cool: "The Pentagon has been hit, too."

"By an airplane?"

"Yes."

"How do you know all this?"

"I've been listening to the shortwave since nine."

"I need to call my wife," he says, moving toward the door. Before reaching it, he turns back to the television. President Bush is walking into a room, but the video feed trembles, freezes and dissolves. The same shot: The President is walking into a room, but, again, the video fails.

"What the fuck is going on?" he asks no one, loudly, before pushing open the door and stumbling into the sunlight.

Charlie and Liv agreed they would speak to each other only on the last Sunday of each month. And each time they spoke, they would "take a reading," as Liv put it, of their marriage. Neither of them had been optimistic about its chances of surviving Charlie's seven and a half months in Guatemala. But they didn't think it necessarily had a greater chance of surviving if he remained in Manhattan. He had a long-anticipated sabbatical from the university where he is an associate professor, and even before their marriage began its swift decline, he'd planned to spend it in Guatemala, researching a book he was writing on Guatemala's civil war.

He and Liv have already had three end-of-the-month conversations. During their last talk, she suggested they see other people. He asked her if she had someone in mind—she said no, although even over the static, he could tell she was lying. His protest, however, was mild—he had slept with Eliza.

He marches across the park, passing the fountain with its stone women spilling water from their breasts, and across the street to the pay phone outside of Un Poco de Todo. Four people are in front of him, and he looks down the street to the Guatel office to see if it might be less crowded. Eliza, who has been silently following him, reads his mind and says she'll look.

The dark-haired woman in front of him is wearing a pair of black jade earrings. When, after a minute, she turns around, he sees how pale she is, as if she'd covered her face in baby powder. "Are you calling New York?" she asks.

"Uh-huh," Charlie says.

"I've been trying since ten this morning. I don't know if the phones are down or too many people are calling or what."

"Is your family in New York?"

"My brother works in the restaurant on top of . . . . The restaurant's called . . . it's . . . . Shit, I can't remember the name."

"Windows on the World?"

She nods. "He's a cook. I don't know if the restaurant is even open in the morning. Is it?"

"I don't know."

"And I don't know if he's supposed to work today anyway. I tried to call my parents, but they live on the upper East Side, so it's the same problem. I can't get anyone."

He wonders if she is going to cry. Instead, she stamps her foot three times, as if crushing a bug. She is wearing black boots. She looks nineteen, but Charlie figures she must be older. If she were nineteen, she'd be in college, another earnest sophomore in his "Central America: Far from Peace, Far from Prosperity" class.

"What about you?" she asks him.

"My wife," he says. "She has a few clients in the towers, but I don't know if she was meeting anyone today." Liv had been a student in his graduate survey. A week before its end, they had, as she later explained to anyone who inquired, "hooked up." When she graduated, she didn't pursue a career in the foreign service, as she'd planned. Instead, she stayed in New York to date him and found abundant work as a Web designer, a field to which she brought considerable creativity and skill but little passion.

Eliza returns, touching him on the shoulder with the same familiar but foreign grip. "There's a notice posted," she says. "'No Calls to New York.' No one could tell me why."

"Thanks," he says. He doesn't look at her but at the lips of the woman in front of him. They are chapped and trembling.

Soon the woman is on the phone, but a minute later, she's off it. "I can't get through," she says. She pounds her foot. "Shit, shit, shit." She is crying.

"Hey," he tells her. "Hey," he says again, more gently, and he reaches toward her, but someone bumps against his back. The line behind him is ten-people long. The girl mumbles a good-bye and disappears.

Eliza is sitting on a bench to his left, out of hearing range. He grabs the phone, puts a twenty-five-centavo piece on the rack above it and punches in the AT&T number. When the operator answers, he gives her Eliza's business number (she works out of their apartment on West 67th Street) and his calling card. "I'll try it, sir," the operator says. No more than three seconds later, she says, "I'm sorry, but I can't get through."

"Could you try it again?"

Seconds later, the operator says, "I'm sorry, sir. Please try again later."

"Could you try again?" he asks, but the line is dead.

The man behind him—he looks Guatemalan—says in halting English, "Our turn, please. Man, sir, it is our turn. Yes?"

But Charlie puts another twenty-five-centavo piece on the rack and dials AT&T again. The result, however, is the same. With quick fury, he smashes the phone against the receiver. When it fails to stick, he picks it up and repeats the gesture. "Fuck you!" he says to the phone. He looks behind him. The line seems to have recoiled, and the Guatemalan man holds his hands over his face, as if Charlie were about to strike him.

Charlie marches to where Eliza is sitting. She has blue-gray eyes, and although he has never found them to be particularly expressive, they now have a watery shine of concern.

"It's okay," she tells him, standing and touching him on the forearm.

"It's not okay," he says. "My wife could be buried under a ton of fucking concrete."

She drops her hand. They stare for a minute out onto the park, which is as crowded as always. *Indígena* girls in ornate *güipiles* and ankle-long *cortes* carry baskets of purses and wallets on their heads, moving from bench to bench, offering their wares to the tourists who lounge as if today were no different than any other day, unmenacing, as mild as the weather.

"We could see if a computer's free at the Rainbow Reading Room," Eliza says. "You could send an e-mail."

"I'm sure half the gringos in Antigua are at the Rainbow Reading Room."

There is a pause before Eliza says, "I know someone. I'd think he'd let you on his computer."

When they are at the door of La Escuela Pan-Americana, across from the La Merced Church, Charlie asks, "Who are we seeing?"

"His name is Hector. He owns the school."

"How do you know him?"

"I studied Spanish here during my first month in the country."

Charlie suspects Eliza slept with Hector. He wonders if he should care.

They wander into a courtyard, its walls lined with bougainvillea, and Eliza leads him toward an office at the back. A woman with long fingernails painted electric blue sits at a desk.

"May I please see Hector?" Eliza says.

"You are a student?" the woman asks.

"A former student."

From behind a door at the back of the office, a man appears. When he sees Eliza, he smiles. He is thinner and taller than Charlie imagined, close to six feet. His skin is honey-colored, and he wears a robust black mustache. His eyes hold steady on Eliza and his smile grows. "More lessons?" he asks her in English.

She crosses past the woman's desk and greets Hector by kissing him on the cheek. For the first time, Hector acknowledges Charlie, giving him a nod.

Eliza turns to Charlie and says, "I'll be right back," and she and Hector step into the back room. He sits in the chair in front of the desk. The woman with the blue fingernails looks at him. "Are you here to study Spanish?" she asks.

"No." He knows he should be more friendly and forthcoming, but he can't help imagining what might have happened: His wife was working this morning on a project at Morgan Stanley or Oppenheimer Funds or another company in the towers.

He tries to hold his focus on the woman's blue nails, but, as if he were staring at a screen in front of him, he sees the North Tower spitting fire and smoke and a jet veer into the South Tower and explode. Although he knows this is a scene a million people—more, many more—have now seen and will remember, perhaps forever, he finds no comfort in the company.

The door at the back opens, and Eliza steps out and motions to him. "He says it's all right," she says. He follows her into a large, square room, lit on two sides by enormous windows. To Charlie's right, Hector sits at an oak desk in front of a Macintosh computer. He pivots in his swivel chair and gives Charlie an indecipherable grin.

"It's online," he says in English. "Ready to go." Hector stands and gestures toward his chair. "All yours, friend."

"Thank you," Charlie says, and, with a fear as visceral as fever, moves quickly to the chair.

A minute later, he is logged onto his AOL account. There are eight new messages, the last one from Liv. He exhales, and relief rides over his fear. His hand, on the computer's mouse, is trembling so much he has difficulty pointing the cursor on Liv's message.

I'm all right, in case you were wondering. I'm sure you were wondering. I'm watching it on TV like the rest of the world. I know dozens of people in both those buildings, Charlie. I'm terrified to think how many of them are dead.

He writes back: *I tried to call. I'm glad you're OK. I was very concerned. Do you want me to come home? I'll be home tomorrow if you want. I can't believe what happened. It sickens me.*

He looks behind him, expecting to see Eliza and Hector, but they have left him alone. There is a strong, pleasant scent in the air—Hector's cologne, perhaps. To the left of the computer is a picture of a Guatemalan girl, no doubt Hector's daughter, seven years old maybe, standing in front of La Merced Church and holding a red balloon. Her hair is long and tangled. He'd call it sexy if she was older.

In a trance, he reads his other messages, one from his mother in Buffalo. She has tried to call Liv, but with no success. He writes to tell her Liv is all right and asks if she'll call Liv's parents in Los Angeles to let them know.

His other messages are dated before today. Five are advertisements, the other is from a former student wanting a letter of recommendation. He wonders how the student found his private e-mail account. He is tempted to refer the student, curtly, to the departmental secretary, who, in turn, will inform him about his sabbatical and unavailability, but after typing a few words, he deletes the message and returns to the mail folder. There are no new messages.

He calls up the *New York Times* Web site. Bin Laden's group is the main suspect, and there was a fourth plane, which crashed south of Pittsburgh.

He tries his message folder again—Liv hasn't replied. He is reluctant to leave the computer, but he wonders what Eliza has promised Hector in return for this favor. Charlie looks again at the picture of Hector's daughter before logging off and returning to the other room. Eliza, waiting for him on the chair in front of the secretary's desk, gives him a sad, questioning glance.

"She's all right," he says.

"Oh," Eliza says, standing. "Thank God."

"I think I need to eat something," Charlie says. "I'm feeling a little on edge." He looks around. "Where did Hector go?"

"To one of the hospitals. Someone who works here, one of the teachers, had an operation last night—appendicitis, I believe he said."

"Should I write him a note, to thank him?"

"It's all right. I'll thank him later."

Charlie tries to read her look, to see what thanking him might entail, but her face tells him nothing.

They return to the sunshine. Across the street, the walls of La Merced Church look as if someone had painted them with fire.

They eat at Vino y Queso under the overhang of a tin roof at the end of a courtyard. Only one other table, at the front end of the courtyard, is occupied, by a long-haired gringo writing in a notebook. A glass of red wine sits in front of him.

The bread comes with real butter, a rarity in the country. But even as he bites into a piece slathered with it, Charlie tastes nothing. His green salad, too, makes no impression on his palate.

"Will you go back to New York?" Eliza asks him.

With his fork, he stabs a piece of lettuce, submerging it in vinegar and oil. "I'm prepared to," he says.

Eliza's hair is tied with a band at the back of her head, but a few strands spill across her cheeks. Her small nose is pink from the sun. He hasn't asked how old she is, and now he thinks she must be younger than he suspected, perhaps in her mid-twenties. She's in Guatemala to volunteer on an archeological dig in the Petén, the northernmost *departamento*, but she hasn't told him when she plans to start.

"I don't know if she'll want me home," he says.

"I would think she would," Eliza says.

"Well, you don't know her. Besides, if I went back now, we would have aborted our trial separation without accumulating enough data to assess our marriage."

Eliza butters a piece of bread and puts a corner of it in her mouth before setting it down. "Do you want to go back?"

"I don't know."

But what he does know is this: He wants Liv to want him back, he wants her to need him. This was why their marriage began to go bad: They didn't need each other. Or, rather, he didn't need her and, before long, she didn't need him. He taught two classes a semester, advised master's students on their theses, did research, wrote. She worked and had weekday drinks and dinners with her single and divorced girlfriends.

As he and Liv were lounging in Central Park one Sunday—they did this as a warm-weather ritual, bringing a blanket, bottled water and the *Times*—she said, "You would probably be just as content alone right now."

His delayed response proved what she'd said true, although he tried a belated protest.

He needed sex, he needed, at times, encouragement when he found himself stuck in his research or writing, he needed someone to listen when he was, as happened a few times a year, simply depressed about the fact of living and its corollary, the fact of dying. When, in a time of rare candidness, he confessed all this to Bill, a colleague, Bill said, "It sounds like you don't need a wife but an occasional whore, cheerleader and shrink."

Bill had, of course, been joking, but Charlie sometimes found himself, during empty moments on the subway or walking across campus after class, thinking Bill was right. This dawning didn't disturb him. Rather, it made him wonder if he had reached a near self-sufficiency, a unilateralism of want.

But in the courtyard of Vino y Queso, he isn't sure anymore what he needs or doesn't need. He feels anger rise in him, a fury against bin Laden or whoever it was who ordered the destruction of the World Trade Center, the carnage at the Pentagon. He'd like to find bin Laden, strap him into the electric chair and pull the switch. He'd like to strangle him with his bare hands. He is used to this kind of rage in himself only in his morning workouts—the vigorous, hour-long weightlifting sessions he does every other day—and when he is drunk and, as always, it surprises him a little.

When, a minute later, the waitress comes with his linguine in clam sauce, he feels his rage subside and the day return to him.

"I think you should go back to New York," Eliza says. "It's the right thing to do. Even if you and your wife don't save your marriage, at least you'll be together for this."

"Don't you want me around anymore?" he asks. He is aware of how flat his voice is, uninflected, cool.

"I never supposed we'd be together long," she says. With a more hopeful tone, she asks, "Did you?"

He didn't. But this isn't what he says. "Maybe you'll go back to Hector."

"Excuse me?"

"You'll go back to fucking Hector."

For a moment, Eliza says nothing. Her eyes are open wide, a startled stare.

I'm sorry, he wants to say. His next words are: "I guess married men are your thing."

Charlie hears the scrape of Eliza's chair as she pushes back from the table. He knows how close she is to leaving—Liv would have been gone by now—and he doesn't want her to.

"First, if you think Hector and I . . . ," she begins. Her nose is red now, like a child's with a cold. He has a sudden urge to wrap his arms around her, to tell her he is sorry, to tell her he loves her and he loves his wife and he is sick, sick to death, about what happened. "Well," she says, "it's none of your concern." She pauses, her brow wrinkled, her eyes narrow. "And if you want to know, Hector isn't married. His wife died a few years ago, died in a bus accident."

"Did he tell you that?" Charlie asks. "It's probably a story he made up to seduce you."

"Jesus Christ, Charlie. He didn't tell me. I hardly know him. The woman I studied Spanish with, Alicia—she told me."

He stabs at his linguine, striking the plate beneath it. *Click. Click. Click.* Eliza stands up, and Charlie feels his heartbeat quicken. He is afraid of what he'll feel when she leaves.

"It's a terrible time, Charlie," she says. "I know you're upset. I'm upset. And I'm scared." She pauses. "If you don't want to go home, I do."

He looks up at her. "I'm sorry," he says. He reaches for his water. He supposes it's cold, but he doesn't feel the glass. "I'm sorry. Will you sit down?" He brings the glass toward him but doesn't drink. "Please?"

At the Rainbow Reading Room, standing under an archway in front of the courtyard, he waits as dusk falls, accompanied by a light rain. This has always been his favorite time of day. It's when, settled over a cup of coffee (two sugars, one half-and-half), he does his best thinking and writing. Early in his marriage, he felt guilty about spending this time at his office, but Liv said she understood. She told him she would make plans to see friends or work late herself. He often worked beyond what was a reasonable dinnertime, even in New York, and Liv adjusted to this, too, dining with her friends. By the time their marriage was a year old, this time was all his, his alone.

When his name is called and he's seated in front of a computer terminal, he taps the *c* on the keyboard three times, but it doesn't register on the screen. He lifts his fist, prepared to slam it on the keyboard, when three *c*'s shoot across the screen. He erases two of them, types his screen name and password (Livlives) and enters his account.

Both Liv and his mother have written. He reads Liv's message first.

Thank you, Charlie, for writing, for being so concerned. I've been outside. It's a beautiful day—the perfect fall day is what all the newscasters are calling it—but it doesn't smell right. Or maybe I'm imagining the smell, thinking about the jet fuel and the debris and the 50,000 people who might be buried alive.

I walked to Riverside Park and saw an old woman on a bench, sobbing. Even before I could move to comfort her, another woman sat beside her and put her arm around her and cried with her. About ten feet from them, I saw a woman in a bikini spread on a huge beach towel, sunbathing. New York, as you can tell, remains the same mix of the sensitive and the self-absorbed.

You asked if you should come home. Certainly a part of me wants you here, to share this. When you are present, Charlie, you are the best company I can imagine.

And I'm scared—no, terrified—wondering when the next plane will hit, where the nuclear bomb might go off.

But here I am, going on and on, avoiding the thesis—an old problem, right?

Here is it: I think you should stay. Air traffic is grounded, and who knows when planes will fly again. Besides, we had a plan, and I guess we should do our best to see it through.

But let's communicate again in a day or two, all right?

Take good care of yourself, Charlie. I'll do the same.

Charlie clicks the reply button and settles his fingers on the keys, tapping the letter *x* steadily, angrily. He thinks she must have someone else to comfort her. He tries to take a deep breath, but his heart races.

He erases the *x*'s and types a line: *Do you have a boyfriend?*

It seems selfish, desperate and petty. He can't say what her life is like now. He wonders when he stopped knowing.

He sees the twin towers—aflame and, then, gone.

He erases the line but can't think what else to write. Finally, he types: *I'm glad you're all right—or as well as you can be. My offer stands—I'll come home immediately if you want.*

The last sentence, he sees immediately, is transparent, his own need to be needed written as if in bold, capital letters. He erases it and writes: *I'll check my e-mail again tomorrow morning. Please let me know what's going on—with the city, with the country but, most important, with you.*

He sends the e-mail, reads his mother's message—she had a long, emotional talk with Liv's mother—and goes first to the *New York Times* Web site, then to the *Washington Post*'s. Already, columnists have weighed in. George Will even makes an allusion to William Wordsworth. Charlie thinks, half in mockery, half in admiration: *Such brilliance at such short notice.* And, a moment later—and quieter—he wonders: *But what does he feel? Isn't he sick, terrified, disgusted? Angry? No—furious?*

He wanders into Mistral, which is crowded but oddly quiet, so quiet he might be at a church service if it wasn't for the muted chatter on the television screen. The TV shows the same pictures, the same collision, the same collapse, and Charlie doesn't reach the bar before he turns around, excuses himself past the crowd of dazed North Americans and Europeans, and heads back into the street. It is no longer raining, and the cobblestones of the wet streets seem to radiate the yellow streetlight.

He walks in the direction of Eliza's apartment and reaches the gate in front of the main house. The gate is open, a surprise, and he steps into the courtyard. On his left, bougainvillea climbs a wall he knows is pink, but without light, it's a muted brown. He walks to the back of the courtyard and knocks on the metal door at the far right. A moment later, Eliza opens it. There is no pleasure in her face, no emotion at all. "Hello," she says. She doesn't step aside or invite him in. "How'd you get inside?"

"The front gate was open."

"Jesus." She is, suddenly, animated.

"I closed it," he says.

"Well, good. I mean, thank you."

"Can I come in?"

"Oh. Well."

Slowly, she steps aside.

He knows this isn't an invitation, but he takes the opening anyway. In the foyer, a fake orchid, which belongs to Eliza's landlady, sits on a stand made of pine.

"Do you want to sit down?" she asks.

"All right," he says. "Thanks." Instead of going into the kitchen or the bedroom, as she normally would, Eliza sits on the unpainted bench on the left side of the foyer. Charlie sits on a wooden stool.

"What's happening?" she asks.

"In the world?"

"I was thinking more about in your life. I believe I know as well as anyone what's going on in the world. I've been listening to the radio all afternoon. Bad news is one of my addictions, it appears. After Princess Di's awful crash, I sat in front of the telly until my eyes turned to tomatoes."

"I didn't figure you as a Princess Di fan," Charlie says lightly.

"I wasn't. Didn't think twice about her when she was alive."

There is a pause before Charlie says, "Liv doesn't want me back." He explains, briefly, about her email message.

"She's only testing you," Eliza says.

"What do you mean?"

"If you go back, she'll know you're serious about your marriage."

"And if I don't?"

Eliza shrugs. "If I were married, I'd want my husband with me in a time like this."

"Even if you didn't like your husband?"

She gives him a soft smile. "Charlie, it's a very frightening time, a time to be with people you love or, if this isn't possible, with people you used to love."

"What about with people you might want to love?" He gives her a questioning glance.

She bites her bottom lip. "Tonight I'm going to stay with a family I know in the capital, a British family. The husband and wife—they both work at the consulate. He's going to pick me up in an hour."

"Oh."

"There are rumors about a terrorist attack here. My landlady said she'd heard talk of armed men—Muslims from the mosque on the Pan-American highway—coming to Antigua to kill gringos."

"That's ridiculous."

"I know, I know. And I'm sure I would be safe here. But at a time like this . . . ." She doesn't finish. She runs a hand over her forehead and across her hair. "I'm sure I'll be back in a day or two, and everything will feel better."

He stands and approaches her. "Eliza," he says, but he doesn't know what else he wants to say.

She is, suddenly, on her feet, moving toward the front door. "I need to pack a few things," she says. She grabs the door handle.

He puts his arms around her chest and pulls her to him, his chest hard against her back. "I'll stay with you tonight," he says, his voice, although soft, too heated, too urgent, to be a whisper. "We'll have dinner. We'll talk."

She struggles to release herself from his embrace, and when she does, she quickly opens the door and steps into the courtyard. There is no moon, there are no stars.

"Please, Eliza," he says, and as if what he said were echoed back to him by the bougainvillea, he hears how pathetic and desperate he sounds. He looks at her, and he hates her because she doesn't love him, doesn't need him. He feels a rush of rage, but Eliza can no longer be its target. She closes her metal door with a snap.

After eating a ham sandwich in his kitchen and listening to President Bush's address on his shortwave radio, he wanders back onto the streets. He stops in front of Cantina Buenafé. Although he has never been inside, he knows its reputation: a place Guatemalans go to drink cheap beer and listen to *ranchera* music on an old record player.

Behind the red curtain guarding the entrance are a handful of round tables, two of them occupied. The record player sits atop what, in another place, might be called an altar. Mixed with the jovial sounds of the *ranchera* music, Charlie hears the muted scratchings of a needle on an LP, a sound familiar from his junior high school days when he used to spend hours listening to the Doors and Pink Floyd and the Rolling Stones. He'd been an awkward teenager—who wasn't?—but he'd found solace in the dark musings of the musicians and he shared their cravings for sex, for delight, for understanding.

He sits at the table nearest the record player, and although he reviles the music, which is played on every bus and in every *tienda* across the country, he anticipates the cool burn of Venado in his throat. For a long time, he waits, gazing at the men at the other tables. They are talking with animation about the day's events—Charlie hears them say "World Trade Center" and "*Los Estados Unidos*" and "Muslims"—but because of the music, little else they say is intelligible.

At last, a thin, long-haired woman comes from a room at the back of the cantina, carrying bottles of beer against her chest. She goes to the table nearest Charlie and distributes them among the four men. She stops at Charlie's table and, looking him over suspiciously, asks what he'd like. He tells her and she retreats into the back room.

He taps his fingers against the table, wondering what he should do. If airplanes aren't flying to the United States, perhaps he could book a flight to Toronto or Montreal and catch a bus into New York. But when he envisions his reunion with Liv, he doesn't see her smiling. He sees the two of them sitting in silence at the table in their box of a kitchen, empty wineglasses and a half-eaten meal in front of them.

He closes his eyes and realizes he is tired, but he doubts he'll be able to sleep. All he sees are the images on the television: the plane, the flames, the collapsing towers.

Gone, he thinks. *Gone. Un-fucking-believable.*

The thin woman brings him an eighth of Venado and a glass. He pours the clear liquid into the glass and drinks. It tastes faintly like rubbing alcohol, but when he's had enough of it, it tastes like nothing.

The thin woman brings him another Venado and, in a minute, it's finished. He'd like to believe he's drunk now—he should be drunk—but he feels, disappointingly, clearheaded.

The needle slides off the record, but instead of returning to the rest position or the beginning of the record, the player's arm remains in the middle of the album. The men at the table nearest his shout protests, but the thin woman is in the back room. When she doesn't return, one of the men steps over to the record player. Charlie recognizes him: Hector. And after he has turned over the record and put the needle on it, he sees Charlie.

He is wearing different clothes than he did earlier: blue slacks and a canary yellow, button-down shirt with thin, vertical blue stripes. The shirt's top two buttons are undone, exposing the top of Hector's hairless chest.

They say hello, and Hector says, in English, "I hope everyone you know is all right."

Instinctively, Charlie nods, although he realizes he could know a dozen people—more—who are dead.

"Good," Hector says. He looks over at his table and asks, "You will join us?"

Charlie is in no mood for company. "Thank you, no." And as if to explain his refusal, he adds, "I'll be leaving soon."

"Okay," says Hector, and he returns to his seat, the *ranchera* music playing again.

Charlie decides he'll leave after one more Venado, and when the thin woman returns, he orders it. The liquor, at last, is beginning to take. His hands and arms feel numb. He thinks: *Tomorrow I'm going to start again. I'm going to rebuild.*

He doesn't know precisely what form his rebuilding will take. He knows he wants to talk to Liv, to explain himself, to tell her he isn't the cold man she thinks he's become. He needs her—it's true, he knows this now.

The thin woman puts another eighth of Venado in front of him, but he doesn't touch it. He'll go back to his apartment and he'll sleep, and in the morning he'll call Liv. When Charlie looks up, Hector is in front of him. The men he was with are gone. "Do you mind if I sit?" he asks, and Charlie points to a chair across from him and says, "Please."

"Bad day," Hector says.

"Yeah, a bad day. A very bad day."

"To do this, they killed themselves, the men who stole the planes—yes?"

"The hijackers? Yeah, they killed themselves."

"They must have been filled with hate."

"Hate?" Charlie shakes his head. "They were crazy—religious fanatics." When Hector doesn't respond, Charlie emphasizes the word by saying *fanaticos*.

As if this were an invitation, Hector speaks Spanish: "But they were acting on behalf of someone, on behalf of people who have suffered because of what your country did?" It isn't entirely a question.

Hector leans back in his chair. Charlie doesn't like Hector's casual tone or the way his lips form a flat, satisfied grin.

"No," Charlie says. As good as his Spanish reading skills are, he has never felt comfortable speaking the language. And even when he isn't drunk, he has trouble finding words. "They're dead. Who knows what they wanted?"

"Yes, they are dead," Hector says, "but people in certain countries are celebrating. The dead men have become martyrs."

In a different place, at a different time, Charlie would be happy to engage in a conversation about perceptions and misperceptions of the United States around the world. But he wonders if Hector is trying to provoke him.

Charlie takes a sip of his Venado. Above the cheerful music, he says, "They're crazy—all of them. Understand?"

Hector says, "You don't think some of them have legitimate grievances?"

"If they do . . . if they do . . . ." Charlie feels the alcohol cloud his head. "Let me tell you, the United States is far more good than bad. We support human rights around the world."

"In Saudi Arabia? In Kuwait?"

"We do in this country," Charlie says, his hand striking the table more forcefully than he'd intended.

"Yes, but only lately and only too late. Where was the United States in the 1980s when Rios Montt was destroying entire villages? It was helping him do it."

"U.S. soldiers never participated in the Guatemalan civil war."

"But U.S. machine guns and grenades did."

The academics from Latin America whom Charlie knows in New York, most of them exiles from El Salvador, Honduras, Peru, and Guatemala, always bemoan the influence the United States wields over their countries, but he never fails to detect envy in their laments.

"It's easy to blame the United States," he says. "It's easier than looking at yourselves and asking what you did wrong."

"But your CIA was here in 1954 to help overthrow our government—yes?"

"Your government would have been overthrown without the CIA," Charlie says. This, in fact, will be one of the major points of his book. Building on the work of Piero Gleijeses, the author of *Shattered Hope*, he'll show how rifts in Guatemala's political and economic classes, with or without the presence of the CIA, would have brought down Jacobo Arbenz.

"Psychologists have a term for this—denial," Hector says.

Charlie feels a powerful urge to grab Hector by the collar of his silly yellow shirt and hurl him against the record player. Although Hector is nearly as tall as Charlie, he must weigh fifty pounds less.

"You speak very critically of the United States," Charlie says. "But your living depends on it."

"Excuse me?"

"Your language school succeeds thanks to students from the United States."

"Most of my students are from Europe," he says. "Students such as Eliza." Hector's smile levitates, broadens, fills with innuendo.

"It's late," Hector says, speaking English again. "It's a long day—yes?"

Charlie wonders where Hector's daughter is and decides she's with her grandparents or an aunt. In Guatemala, children are raised by the proverbial village. Charlie remembers discussing having children with Liv during the blissful, theoretical days of their courtship.

"I am sorry about your country," Hector says. And, after a pause, he adds, "Now you know."

"Know what?" Charlie asks, but in answer, Hector gives him only a small smile. Hector says goodbye, but he makes no move to shake Charlie's hand and Charlie doesn't stand to do so. After he watches Hector leave, Charlie drops a twenty-quetzal bill on the table and follows him into the night.

The air is cool and rain-softened. Whatever effect the alcohol had on Charlie is gone. He is stunned and frustrated by his sobriety. Twenty feet ahead of him, he sees Hector walking on the sidewalk in staggered paces. He is drunker than he seemed at the cantina.

On the deserted cobblestone street, only every third streetlight works. The walls and doors of the houses abutting the sidewalk look dismal and gray.

With quick steps, Charlie closes the distance between himself and Hector. Even with Charlie a step behind him, Hector doesn't turn around. Hector is mumbling or singing or perhaps cursing—yes, almost certainly cursing, Charlie thinks, cursing him, cursing the United States.

Charlie doesn't announce himself, but with a swift pounce grabs Hector beneath the armpits and thrusts him against the hard facade to his left, a heavy wooden door. Hector shouts in surprise and pain, and pleased with this reaction, Charlie repeats the assault, this time with twice the fury. He feels Hector's head meet the wood and hears—or thinks he hears—the sound of Hector's skull cracking or teeth shattering.

Hector struggles, thrashing his elbows, but he is like a trout at the bottom of a fishing boat, his movements only a futile precursor to stillness.

Again, Charlie prepares to smash Hector's head against the door, and he feels himself fill with the beginnings of a triumphant yell—payback, vengeance, they are his now—when the door swings open and on the threshold appears a girl with long, tangled dark hair. She is twelve years old or ten or younger, and in the poor streetlight, Charlie cannot see much besides her hair and her eyes, open in sudden terror and fear, but fixed on him, understanding him in a way he cannot understand himself, her gaze hard and unblinking, as if to keep him in her sights forever.

Because of the walk, half a kilometer up a long hill under a sky about to give way to rain, Iris should have let someone know she was coming, sent a telegram, telephoned. But to have announced herself would have defeated her purpose. So, after the *ayudante* pulls her suitcase from beneath the Pullman and deposits it beside her on the side of the highway, and after the bus pulls away—it's a new bus, although it spits black smoke back at her like the busses she remembers—she is left to wonder how she'll make it into town. She lifts her suitcase, whose wheels broke somewhere in transit from Miami to Guatemala City, but quickly drops it. When she lived here thirty years ago, she would have been able to carry the suitcase up the hill. But she wouldn't have had a suitcase, which is black and made of polyester and vinyl and designed to fit in the overhead bins of airplanes. She would have had a knapsack, and she would have walked up the hill without breathing heavily, without noticing the climb at all.

She feels the first drops of rain, a mist-like rain, *chipi-chipi*, and she looks around for shelter. Behind her is what, on first glance, she supposed was a shack. Thirty years ago, it would have been. Looking closely, she sees it's a gray block building with glass windows, an electric cash register and, at the back, a line of glass-doored refrigerators.

Dragging her suitcase across the gravel, Iris is halfway to the store, which is empty save the girl sitting on a stool behind the cash register, when a car pulls beside her. On the driver's side door of the baby blue Corolla, in black, cursive letters, is the word *Taxi*. The driver, who looks no older than twelve—his face is pudgy, as if from baby fat, and his eyes have a bright quality she associates with children—leans out of his window and says in English, "Would you like a ride?"

On returning to Santa Cruz Verapaz, where she'd lived for eighteen months three decades ago, she had expected to recognize everyone, expected—fancifully, ridiculously, she now realizes—the town to have remained unchanged, as it has in her photographs and memory. She doesn't recognize the taxi driver nor the girl in the store, and she knows it would be miraculous if she did because they wouldn't have been born when she lived here. Nevertheless, they might have reminded her of their parents, and so she might have known their lineage, if not their names. But the driver and the girl in the store don't look at all familiar, and she is disappointed by this, even crestfallen. She'd been hoping her first encounter in her old town would have been with someone she knew. She'd imagined telling the person—it would be a woman, perhaps one of the two she'd worked with at the health center—her bad news and, when the surprise of it had sunk in, receiving her elaborate, tearful sympathy.

Iris responds to the driver's invitation with a smile and a "Si, por favor," and he sweeps up her bag and deposits it in his trunk. She settles into the passenger seat. The driver says, "My name is Roberto. Where are you going?"

"Posada La Esperanza." She adds, "If it still exists."

"Oh yes," Roberto says, and he revs his engine and bolts onto the highway before making a quick left turn up Calle Tres de Mayo, Santa Cruz's main street.

Roberto waits with her at Posada La Esperanza until the heavy oak door is opened by a tall, pale woman with high cheek-bones and greenish-gray eyes. Iris had been expecting the old proprietress, Doña Esperanza, although she'd been ancient when Iris knew her and must be dead a decade at least.

"How may I help you?" asks the woman, and Roberto speaks before Iris can: "She'd like a room."

"With a private or public bath?"

"Private," Iris says. When she first came to Santa Cruz, she rented a room here and shared a bathroom with Gertrude, a German who was completing a dissertation on migrant coffee workers. At the end of every day, Gertrude took half-hour-long showers, although the water was never anything but arctic.

"Come in," says the woman, and Iris pays Roberto, who says, "When you are ready to leave, she will call me"—he indicates the woman—"and I will drive you back to the crossroads to meet your bus."

"Thank you."

"And," Roberto says, "if you would like a tour of Cobán or San Cristóbal—or even Lanquín—I am at service to you."

"Thank you, but I know the area well. At least, I used to."

The woman introduces herself as Leti and asks Iris to write her name and nationality next to the date in a spiral notebook. Iris notices that the pensión has had no guests in the last week. She had been hoping—again irrationally, fancifully—to meet Gertrude here, to listen to her critique the boyfriends she'd left behind in West Berlin. But they would no longer be boyfriends— they would be ex-husbands—and she would no longer be hailing from West Berlin but Berlin.

Leti shows Iris her room. It's on the second floor above a brick courtyard. Its two windows open to a half-moon-shaped balcony with a three-foot-high iron railing. In the center of the room is a double bed with a single pillow.

"This will be all right?" Leti asks, and Iris nods.

Leti's voice is high and girlish, nothing like Doña Esperanza's, which was deep and grave, a contrast to her shrunken, ninety-pound body. "Is Doña Esperanza still alive?" Iris asks.

Leti's smile leaves her face. "My grandmother died when I was five. I remember her. She used to eat a grape *helado* every night, and if my brothers and I were good, we could have a lick—only a lick. You knew her?"

Iris begins to tell the story of how, when she first came to town, she stayed here until she could find a permanent place and sat with Doña Esperanza every evening to discuss the weather. "One evening," she says . . . . But Leti seems to have lost interest in the conversation, her eyes wandering around the room, and when Iris concludes her remembrance prematurely, Leti sighs with relief.

Iris will not let Leti go before she asks, "Do you know Victor Catalán?"

"The father or the son?"

"By now, it would be the father."

"He lives on *primera calle*, in the green house."

Iris knows Victor's green house well. Thirty years ago, she lived next door to it.

"So he is married?" Iris asks.

Leti says, "His wife lives in the United States. She comes here twice a year, for Christmas and Semana Santa." Leti is obviously more interested in this conversation than the one about her grandmother. "Is he your friend?" She says the last word with suspicion.

"An old friend," Iris says.

Leti lingers, as if expecting more, but when Iris isn't forthcoming, Leti excuses herself. Iris unpacks, placing her clothes on top of the bed. She plans to stay four days. Two days after her return to the States, she will begin treatment at the Cleveland Clinic. Isabel, her daughter, will stay with her at the Guest House, monitoring her fevers and securing icepacks on her thighs and stomach. Iris is fifty-three years old, and before her cancer, her only affliction had been a broken leg, the result of falling off a horse when, after her divorce, she spent a summer in Wyoming.

For as far back as she knows the history, everyone in her family, men and women alike, plodded dutifully into old age. So when, a year ago, she'd discovered blood in her urine, she'd chalked it up, fancifully, to an aberrant period, a stray egg shooting down her womb three years after menopause. But her gynecologist, to whom she'd mentioned the incident, had had her see a specialist. The cancer had been confined to one kidney. The doctor who removed the diseased kidney said her cancer was, more than likely, gone forever, dispatched under the quick cure of the knife. It wasn't. A year later, the cancer had spread to her lungs.

During the first manifestation of her cancer, she'd spent long hours on the phone with Isabel. She'd received cards and phone calls from her friends. Even Curtis, her ex-husband, with whom she hadn't communicated in half a decade, wrote her a note. After her kidney was removed, she accepted the doctor's optimistic words as truth rather than projection, and she'd planned the rest of her life in a trio of fulfilling, ten-year blocks.

When her cancer returned, the doctor had had a less cheerful prognosis: Three out of every four patients whose cancer spreads beyond the kidney don't live more than two years. The treatment, a combination of two drugs, often has debilitating side-effects. "Do what you need to do before your treatment starts," he advised. For three days, she was stunned into inactivity and muteness, staying home from work and calling no one. At last, she informed Isabel. And, the same evening, she planned this trip.

She'd come here thirty years ago after signing on with a U.S.-government-sponsored relief program a month after she graduated with a health education degree from Mount Holyoke. It was the first time she'd ever been outside the United States, and although she was certain she would live in other, even more remote and beautiful places, she hadn't. Upon her return to the States, she'd met Curtis and they'd had Isabel and moved to Washington, D.C., where the world had come to them.

She is aware of the danger of returning to Santa Cruz. Someone viewing her trip from a distance might see it as a doomed flirtation with nostalgia. In her mind, however, she had played down her expectations, reminding herself of how long ago she'd lived here and how time might have deepened and exaggerated the pleasures she'd experienced.

What she remembers: In the evenings, the sky opened up, pushing aside the clouds and leaving a rich expanse of azure. She used to meet Victor in the park on his return from classes at San Carlos University in Cobán, the nearby large town. They would sit on high stools in front of Tienda Luz and drink Coca-Colas and talk lazily, as if the evening would stretch as long as the sky, about what they'd done during the day, what village Iris had gone to and whether the women there had been receptive to what she'd told them about breast-feeding and the importance of vegetables and fruits in their diets. Victor didn't talk much, but when he did, it was usually to make fun of his agriculture professors, old men in tailored suits who'd spent their lives toiling in greenhouses and strolling the rows of model farms instead of working in the *campo,* where farmers planted where they could—on perilous slopes, by streambeds—and were lucky if they had a bag of fertilizer or a quart of pesticide to last the season.

On one especially warm evening, they'd gone to the river on the west side of town. They'd expected it to be crowded and it was, with two dozen schoolboys cooling themselves after a day in hot classrooms, but Iris and Victor had outlasted them and the sunset. In the cooling darkness, they found each other in chest-deep water. She placed her hands around Victor's neck and wrapped her legs around his waist. She wasn't much lighter than he was—he was taller than she by three inches, but he had a boy's thin, smooth body—and he never could have supported her like this on land. She knows their encounter had probably been brief. Their eagerness and the illicitness of what they were doing had probably excited Victor beyond his usual excitement. Yet she remembers their union as long, languid even, with time to feel everything—the pulse of the river against her side, the cool breath of the breeze on her back, Victor's hardness finding its familiar, deep place inside her.

She'd bought a cheese sandwich in the capital, and after she eats it in the courtyard, she walks outside. The rain has stopped, although the sky is muddied with gray clouds. She walks down Calle Tres de Mayo, which was a dirt road when she lived here but is now a paved thoroughfare. She greets people as she walks, and they give her pleasant smiles, but she doesn't recognize a single face.

In front of the indoor market, *indígena* women sit with their baskets of tomatoes and onions. She stops in front of a long-faced woman with thin, smoke-colored hair. "Tortillas?" the woman asks her.

"Dos, por favor," Iris says. The woman hands her two warm tortillas, their texture like skin.

There is something familiar about the woman's face, the thin length of it, and Iris asks, "Have you always sold your tortillas here?"

The woman looks up at Iris, squinting despite the lack of a sun. "Sí, Señora."

"For how long?" Iris asks.

"Years."

"I lived here thirty years ago. I used to buy tortillas every day at the market, and on many days I must have bought them from you."

The woman nods and even gives Iris a hint of a smile, a thin line across her mouth.

"Do you have a daughter?" Iris asks. "I remember seeing you with a little girl."

"I have three sons."

"Oh," Iris says. "Wonderful."

She hears the rain murmuring on tin roofs before she feels it. The women who are sitting beyond the reach of the market's roof cover what they're selling with clear sheets of plastic.

"Thank you for the tortillas," Iris says. "I will enjoy them."

"*Vaya bien*," the woman says and pulls plastic over her basket.

Iris lifts the blue hood of her raincoat over her head. Covered up, she looks no different from the other people on the street, who have protected themselves from the rain in one way or another. She eats her tortillas. Already they have turned lukewarm, and while they taste better than the flour tortillas she is used to in the States, she remembers them having a richer texture, their flavor hinting at the wood they were cooked over.

She continues down the street, and before it dips toward the highway, she turns right. At the bottom of the street, on the left, is the Centro de Salud. It is made of concrete block, and its light green paint is fresh. She pulls open the glass door. Bright neon light fills the main room. The pair of rooms on both her right and left are closed, but the office at the back is open, and at its lone desk sits Blanca Oralia. She is wearing a pair of red-framed glasses, and her face, large when Iris knew her, seems to have grown to the size of a pumpkin.

"Yes, Señora?" Blanca says. "How may I help you?"

Iris takes a few steps toward her. "Blanca," she says. "I am Iris Merchant. I used to work with you and Marisa García."

By the expression on Blanca's face, Iris knows she needn't have provided the explanation. Blanca has recognized her, and Iris feels a rush of warmth, of homecoming.

Blanca comes around her desk and embraces her. "Hello, Irena," she says.

Iris is tripped up by Blanca's misunderstanding. "No, it's Iris," she says. "Like a rainbow, remember—arco-*iris*."

Blanca breaks her embrace. "Iris? Yes, like the rainbow, of course. I remember, I remember." She smiles. "You have come back."

"Yes."

"To work?"

"No, to visit."

"Good. What do you think of Santa Cruz now?"

"It is different than I remember."

For several minutes, they talk about the changes in the town, a pleasant exchange Iris might have with a stranger.

Iris says, "Does Marisa still work here?"

"She left ten years ago to go to the States."

Iris says, "Do you remember how the three of us were walking to Pambach to give vaccinations to children and how we found six bottles of beer cooling in the stream?"

"Yes," Blanca says, and Iris detects relief in her voice, the relief of someone finding a familiar trail after tramping miles in the woods. "Marisa wanted to drink them all."

"And I said we should drink only one, to spare the poor farmer the bad luck of finding all his beer gone."

"We shared a bottle," says Blanca.

"And even after one beer . . . "

" . . . we found ourselves drunk."

They both laugh, and Blanca hugs her again, as if to make up for her earlier forgetfulness.

"And do you remember how the three of us visited Las Serenitas to offer treatment to the girls?" Blanca asks. "Marisa instructed the proprietress on how she should decorate the rooms—use blue curtains instead of red, paint the walls yellow instead of pink, and have a basket of condoms by the front door. And this was before anyone had heard of AIDS!" Blanca begins to laugh, but pauses to read Iris's face. Iris wasn't a part of this whorehouse adventure. Determined to pretend, however, she smiles and says, "Marisa had her ideas, didn't she?"

"She was *loca*," Blanca agrees, and they both laugh, although it isn't the robust laugh of earlier.

Blanca doesn't share another anecdote. Instead, she says, as if in apology, "Many *gringas* have worked here. They come for a year, two sometimes, then return to their countries. I have photographs."

She steps over to her desk and from a bottom drawer removes a fistful of pictures. They are in both color and black and white, and Blanca spreads them in front of her. She begins to narrate what is in one when Iris interrupts: "Here I am!" The picture she picks up is of Blanca, Marisa, and herself standing in front of a waterfall. Whoever took the picture was standing at a distance, and the three figures in the photo look tiny and thin juxtaposed against the giant stream of water cascading off a mountain rock behind them.

"I remember," Blanca says, again with relief. "This is when we went to Lanquín."

Iris did go to Lanquín once, but it was with Victor. They camped below the Lanquín caves and spent the evening watching bats hunt insects over the nearby stream. Later, in their tent, it was so dark they couldn't see each other, and, in a ghost-story whisper, Victor told her the tale of La Llorona, the *indígena* mistress of

Cortez who, ashamed to have conceived with a Spaniard, drowns their baby and forever afterwards haunts the streets, weeping as she searches for the body of her dead child.

When Iris inspects the faded photograph closely, she sees that the woman, although blond and tall, isn't her. It is Irena, perhaps, or another of the women who have come to Santa Cruz, however briefly, to lend her expertise and enthusiasm.

"Lanquín is beautiful," Iris says. "Do you go often?"

"In the past, I would go two or three times a year. But in recent years, no. I am too old to climb to the waterfalls."

"I understand."

"Are you feeling well?" Blanca asks after a pause. "You look tired."

"I came from the capital this morning."

"It is a long trip. Perhaps you would like to rest now."

"I think I would."

"You will come back tomorrow?"

Iris knows Blanca's question is sincere, yet she wonders what more they would have to talk about. It was Marisa with whom she felt more comfortable. It was Marisa who sat up with her on certain nights, drinking rum and Coke and cautioning her about dating a Guatemalan man.

"I will come back tomorrow," Iris says. "Good-bye, Blanca."

"Good-bye, Irena." Blanca catches herself, blushes and pats Iris companionably on the shoulder. "Iris, I mean. Iris like the rainbow."

In her bed in La Posada Esperanza, Iris tries to nap. Although her room isn't directly above Calle Tres de Mayo, as some are, she nevertheless hears the grumble of busses and the loud revving of car engines. She thinks about Victor and what he might have done in the past thirty years. She wonders if he ever completed his doctorate. She wonders about his wife and why she, rather than he, went to the United States. Usually, it is the husband who braves the illegal, overland journey, rooms with other men in cramped apartments and faithfully express-mails money home. She wonders how he will react to her visit, wonders if her presence will stir up his anger at her leaving him long ago. She knows, but can barely admit to herself, that what she wants is to see if he still has feelings for her, however muted by time.

She spends another restless forty-five minutes in bed before rising and brushing her hair. There is no mirror. She stares at her faint reflection in the two windows in front of the room. She wishes she had dyed her hair. The broad swaths of silver in her otherwise blond, shoulder-length hair make her seem older than she is. And she wishes she hadn't, in an effort to recreate the guileless, simple life she'd known, left her make-up behind. She could have covered the brown spots on her temples, she could have rouged her cheeks and whitened her neck. To meet the past, she decides, she should have tried her best to look as she did in it.

"Yes, Señora?"

Iris feels she is looking at Victor as in a funhouse mirror. He is the same man she knew, with the same thick black hair, the same dark eyes, but he seems to have become both shorter and wider, as if, like a clay doll, he'd been flattened by a cruel fist from above. He is standing in the doorway of his house, she is on the front stoop. There is no light above her, and this, she thinks, is why he doesn't recognize her.

She'd prepared a joke, something offhanded and casual—"I happened to be in town, and I thought I'd say hello"—but his failure to recognize her spoils this, and she says, "I'm Iris. Iris Merchant."

When, at last, he grasps who is in front of him, his apprehension comes without the flash of joy she'd believed she might bring him. She realizes her entire trip had been planned around this moment. Now the moment has happened— blandly.

"Iris, please, *pase adelante*," he says, and he pushes the door open and steps aside. Even as she's crossing the threshold, she wishes she was back in her room at Posada La Esperanza—no, she wishes she was back in the States, imagining this scene instead of living it.

"Please, come this way," he says. He steps to his left, into his living room, and indicates the white couch against the wall. "Sit down, please."

"Thank you, Victor. I came because . . . I wanted to see how you are."

"I have finished dinner. Otherwise, I would invite you to eat with me. The *muchacha* is still cleaning up in the kitchen.

Perhaps she could make you something—some cabbage soup or chicken and rice."

"I ate dinner, Victor. Thank you." She didn't eat dinner; she hadn't been hungry and she isn't hungry now.

"Coffee?" Victor asks.

"Yes, please."

Victor leaves, and Iris walks to the end of the room to a mahogany cabinet with a glass door. Inside are a dozen or so framed photographs. It takes Iris a full minute to spot Victor's wife because she hadn't expected this: She is a white woman, a *gringa*, as blond and tall as Iris, although heavier and with broader shoulders. Her nose is long—it doesn't, however, strike Iris as unattractive.

Iris settles onto the white couch as Victor returns with the *muchacha*, a thin girl of about fifteen. She is carrying a cup of coffee and a plate with three pieces of sweet bread. She places them on the table in front of the couch and returns to the kitchen.

Victor sits in the white armchair across from her. Behind him is a television. Above it, on the wall, is a cheap weaving. *Recuerdo de Lanquín* is embroidered in white over its purple background.

Victor asks her what she thinks of Santa Cruz, and they talk, as she and Blanca did, about changes in the last thirty years.

Iris says, "Your house is the same."

"It is the same as when my mother lived here. When she died, Hilda, my wife, wanted the rooms painted different colors. But when Hilda moved back to the States, I painted the rooms again the colors they were. I knew my mother's ghost would be satisfied." He smiles, a smile she doesn't recognize. It isn't his schoolboy smile, the kind he exhibited after critiquing his professors. This smile is small and reserved, the corners of his mouth barely turning up, as if the effort were too much.

Victor's eyes are heavy and puffy. A crescent of blue is under each. His breathing seems labored, a smoker's breathing. She wonders if he is ill. She hadn't foreseen this: a reunion of ex-lovers becoming a tete tête-à-tête of invalids. When she thought of this moment, she'd envisioned alternate scenarios, one in which she told him about her cancer, one in which she didn't. Now she can foresee her confession dovetailing into his, the two of them engaging in the kind of medical talk she endures from her parents, both of whom are in their late seventies and likely to outlive her.

"Are you and your wife divorced?" she asks Victor.

He shakes his head. "She was tired of her work here."

"What was her work?"

"She was an instructor at the University of San Carlos, training nurses to work in the rural areas of Guatemala. It was hard work and they paid her very little. With my salary, however, it was enough. But with both young Victor and Anna in college, we had more expenses. So she found a job at a hospital in Oklahoma."

"You couldn't go with her?"

"What work could I do in Oklahoma? I have a good job here. I am an agronomist with DIGESA. Every day I work with farmers in the *campo*. In Oklahoma, I would be sweeping floors. But . . . ." He pauses. "But only two days ago, my wife called to tell me about a job in Oklahoma working with families from Mexico and Honduras and, yes, Guatemala. They are migrant farmers, and I would make sure they were treated fairly by their employers and had enough medical care. Coordinator of Migrant Worker Services is the title of the job. Hilda knows the director of the agency, and he said he would be glad to have me."

He looks around the room, and she follows his gaze to the framed picture of Jesus, a shepherd's staff in his hand, on the wall next to the far window, the pair of brown leather shoes in the corner, the three white candles burned to stubs on the side table next to the couch. They are parts of his accumulated life. So, too, is she, although she understands now how insignificant her place in it is. And so, too, is his place in hers. Since she was last in this room, she has filled three decades. No matter how frivolously she might have spent them—and she didn't, the Hispanic women's programs she developed at the National Institute of Health and Isabel are two proofs of this—they would, by their sheer span, have made her eighteen months here, no matter how full of passion and discovery, seem small.

"For a job alone, I would never leave my country," he says. "But my wife and I see each other only twice a year. She says she misses me. And, yes, I miss her." He looks at Iris squarely. For a moment, she sees him as he was: his face thin, his eyes vivid and without the underlines of years and distress. For a time in their lives, he felt as deeply about her as anyone in his life. But how can she be certain of this? Emotion leaves no trace—it is swept into time more cleanly than the smallest object.

"I know it can't be easy to leave Guatemala," she says.

Victor smiles, a smile closer in spirit to the one she knew. "Remember: I wouldn't even leave for you."

"Did I ask you to?" She poses the question without irony. She doesn't remember ever seriously discussing Victor coming to the United States with her.

"You talked about it one time," he says. "I don't think I gave you the response you were expecting, and you didn't mention it again."

"So you weren't angry when I left?"

"Angry? Don't you remember how I carried your bags to the crossroads at the end of Calle Tres de Mayo? You were crying so much I was worried you would faint."

Iris remembers a different parting. She had come to his house, this house, to say good-bye and sat with him and his mother in this very room. Victor, his arms wrapped around his chest, had averted his gaze, and she had listened to his mother bemoan her sickness, whatever sickness it was. When she left, Victor hadn't even stood up. It was his mother who shuffled to the door to see her go.

Is this how they said good-bye? Or could her visit with Victor and his mother have occurred at another time, perhaps after they'd had an argument and hadn't yet reconciled? Her doctors told her the cancer treatment might impair her memory, but they'd mentioned nothing about the cancer itself doing this.

"And," Victor says, "a few months later, Hilda came to town. Like you, she came to work in the Centro de Salud. She rented your old house." He says this with a hint of triumph, as if to show her her leaving hadn't hurt him if he was soon open to another woman's love.

But she cannot allow him to dismiss what they shared. "Did you ever go to the river with her?" She knows her question is bold, even impolite, but it is her last chance to live with him again in the place they were.

"The river?" he asks.

She feels foolish, shameless, desperate, as if she were prodding him into an affair he didn't want. He will, it seems, leave her all alone in the river, the water sweeping past her.

But he surprises her with a gentle laugh. "To swim, yes." He laughs again. "But only to swim."

They both laugh now, and after this, their conversation follows easily, harmlessly, across the landscape of their pasts.

A dream wakes Iris when it is still dark and all the street sounds have quieted. She dreamed she died lying on a cot, the kind of canvas cot the Centro de Salud used to have. Isabel knelt over her. Iris could tell by her daughter's expression how confused she was. *She's dead,* she could see her daughter thinking. *What do I do now?*

Iris tried to explain the next steps—contact the supervising nurse, call the funeral home, send a notice to the newspaper—but she knew she was dead and was, therefore, unable to speak. She tried anyway; nothing came out of her mouth. *My God,* Iris thought, *I should have told her I was dying. I should have told her what dying means.*

She leaves her bed and walks to the windows at the front of the room and stares at the square of sky above the courtyard. Between gray strands of clouds, she sees stars.

What a small thing a life is compared with the universe, she thinks. She pictures her life as a white bird flying toward the star she is gazing at now. How close to the star would her white bird reach in even a hundred years, even if it flew as fast as light? It would only be at the beginning of its journey. It would barely have left the earth.

The waterfalls of Lanquín are terraced into pools, each pool ending in a cascade with another pool below it. Three quarters of the way down the falls, the water splits. On one side, the water pours into a pool, which, like the preceding pools, ends in a cascade, its water continuing a gradual descent into the river basin. On the other side is a cave, its opening perhaps five times the size of a laundry basket, into which water rushes at great speed. Sitting on a smooth, wet rock above the cave, Iris remembers the rumor of how a despondent lover threw himself into the cave, his body swallowed whole. For her, however, the cave always had a different resonance than despair and death. It had seemed the essence of sexuality, its gaping opening receiving the wild flow of water and the water, so people said, never resurfacing but rushing straight to the center of the earth.

Even on a hot day such as today, it is cool near the cave because of the mist rising out of it. Iris sees now how frightening this place is, how, if she isn't careful, she could slip down the side of the rock and shoot the rapids into the cave and eternity. But even now, she sees the cave as more life than death, the great rush of water like desire, like the will to live. *God*, she thinks, *it's wonderful to see this again.*

In the pool below her, Roberto is standing, the water to his waist. He'd driven them the four hours from Santa Cruz, and because his Corolla couldn't handle the uneven, muddy road up to the waterfall, he'd parked off the town square in Lanquín and they'd walked. Iris didn't feel as winded as she thought she would, and she told him, "You'd think someone with cancer would be throwing up in the bushes by now." It had happened as easily as this, her revealing her news to someone here, in the country she'd loved, and he said, incredulously, "You have cancer?" She explained and he listened and showed concern. Perhaps his was the concern of someone she was paying to lead her on an excursion, but she didn't think so. He was only a boy, sixteen years old, and he wasn't awake yet to the world's sorrows. In his eyes, every misfortune was unfair, an injustice, and not yet simply the sad way of the world.

They'd talked about other things, too, such as why he wasn't in school (he couldn't afford it and he was looking after his sick mother) and whether he planned to marry one day (when he was thirty, so he could first go to the United States to make his fortune).

"Let me see you swim," Iris calls to him.

Roberto shakes his head. "I don't know how to swim."

Iris looks again at the cave, gaping, omnivorous. She imagines hurling herself into it. Such a death would be swifter and more merciful than what likely faces her. But most deaths, like most births, are filled with agony. Given the pain at the beginning and end of life, one would think that what falls between them would be all happiness, a ride on slow-moving water. Some of it is, of course. The first time she and Curtis kissed. The way Isabel, when she was a toddler, used to dance on the wood floor of the living room, twirling, a self-propelled merry-go-round, laughing until she fell down. This cave and its ferocious, beautiful water.

"Well," she shouts down to Roberto, "I'll have to teach you."

Iris walks around the cave and down a slope into the pool

where Roberto, his red shorts pulled above his belly button, awaits the instruction of a stranger who is less strange now, who will, after three days, come to seem almost familiar.

"You'll come back, won't you Iris?" Roberto asks. "You'll see, I'll swim the full length of the pool in Lanquín." Roberto is driving her to the bus stop at the crossroads in Santa Cruz. Like the good driver he is, he is keeping his eyes on the road. Yet even from her imperfect vantage point in the passenger seat, she sees the brightness in them, the spark of innocent bravado.

"I'd like to come back," she says. "And maybe I will."

"Bring Isabel with you. I will invite you to my house. My mother will be well and she'll prepare . . . ." He continues enthusiastically, but she only half listens. Her attention is focused on the song playing on his cassette deck. She has heard it several times in the past three days as they've driven to Lanquín, Cobán, San Cristóbal. Although it has no words, it is her favorite song on the tape. Two guitars respond to each other like courting lovers—flirtatious, seductive and, at the end, mournful, as if they're saying good-bye.

They are nearly at the bus stop. The song is over. Iris says, "Roberto, I have a favor."

"Yes?"

"Will you play that song again, the song we just heard?"

"Oh, yes." He pauses. "Well . . . my tape player is broken. Only the play button works. I could flip the tape, play it on the other side, put it in again, and . . . "

"No, that's all right," she says. And it is all right. It has to be. Besides, she'll remember the song. She'll hum it all the way home. "Anyway, look. Here's my bus."

The bus pulls onto the shoulder of the road, its front windshield tinted, only the driver's hands on the wheel visible.

Iris says, "It's early."

Mark Brazaitis is the author of *The River of Lost Voices: Stories from Guatemala*, winner of the 1998 Iowa Short Fiction Award, and *Steal My Heart*, a novel published in 2000. He is a past recipient of a National Endowment for the Arts fellowship, and his stories, poems and essays have appeared in *The Sun*, *Witness*, *Beloit Fiction Journal*, *Confrontation*, *Notre Dame Review*, and *Shenandoah*. He is an assistant professor of English at West Virginia University.